Michael Coleman

BRIGHT RIPPLES
IN A DARK POOL

Number   *C900038899*

Class

Original Title: BRIGHT RIPPLES IN A DARK POOL
Michael Coleman © 2013
© 2013 Editorial Seleer
info@editorialseleer.com
www.editorialseleer.com
Impreso en España / Printed in Spain
Printed by EDITORIAL SELEER (PUBLISHING GROUP) 2013
Lay-out: Girón Canseco Cynthia D.
1ª edition
ISBN: 978-84-942104-2-6
Legal Deposit: MA 2230-2013
Impresión: Estugraf Impresores

BRIGHT RIPPLES
IN A DARK POOL

CONTENTS

For all the wonderful ripples in my pool ! ~ Michael Coleman

A FABLE?

"for the good are always merry, save by an evil chance" W.B. yeats

A FABLE ?

The Alley.

"The boy was not simple, he was – naive. Just naive. Too honest for this 'ere life we's a leading." The speaker was a hulk of a man, and he was there - as in there he is - and no mistake; the universe had a place for him and he most certainly filled it. His mouth was unseen behind a rowdy, curling beard. The beard was part of a gush of red curls tumbling in disarray all around his head. He was tall and broad and wrapped in layers of ragged clothes. The clothes and the fiery hair dominated his appearance. Both added to his bulk and the flimsy pieces of loose cloth, hanging on by threads to the remnants of coats, trousers et al, moved with his slightest movement. This flow of scrim and tatters animated, in a graceful way, his typical big man awkwardness. There was an awful lot of him and his hairy frame practically filled the alley. He was like an ancient and fearsome god standing there by the fire - a hammerless Thor, glowing orange in the melodically, shifting light. His companions called him, naturally enough it seemed - Big Red. When he had joined this community he had offered a born name, but born names have history; and place; and memory, attached. Memory is often a heavy burden. And born names in this place are always associated with loss. So it is an unwritten rule in this society that they are immediately dispensed with. A street name means something else. It is not a nickname; it is a new name – for a new life. It was always something that fitted - like a label, sometimes cruel, sometimes humorous, even ironic, sometimes it was even beautifully poetic – but it always fitted.

Red had known the boy better than anyone else there. Though the boy was not much more than a child, Red had been enriched by the knowing of him.

"Simple or naive don't matter now. Got big trouble for 'is self and started big trouble for us all. Big bloody trouble". As he spoke Hunchy cleaned a long drip from his bony nose with a shiny, filthy sleeve. He paused, lifted his arm and examined the freshly glistening track for a moment by the firelight, as if he was trying to read it. If so he obviously found nothing of interest and he went on. "Damn stupid brat. Big trouble that's what we 'as now."

"Did'e leave a roll? Does anybody know did'e leave a roll or anything?" Spluttered Rainman excitedly. Droplets of his sprayed spit shone fleetingly in the flame-light. The pitiful fool was all teeth, and bulging, idiot eyes. He would have had last pickings if there had been something left.

"Nobody touches his roll." Growled Red.

"Wants it all for yerself. Does ya?" sneered Hunchy. Red ignored him, he considered Hunchy's mind as twisted as his spine.

"He'd a give ya anythin that boy. Wud'na saw ya stuck. They'll whip him ya know, they'll whip him" Cried Skinny Minny through a dirty hanky. She was dabbing her running nose and tearful eyes with the damp rag. A skin-like pallor showed where her tears and snot had allowed a little of her grime to rub onto the hanky. Occasionally she tilted her head and theatrically pushed a lousy strand of stringy hair behind her ear. An old habit. There was a time when she could tantalise a bar-room full of men by the same simple action. In those days her shining hair would bounce gently and slowly to her touch, reflecting the rooms light with a fiery display of copper flashes. Her eyes too would sparkle with the bright promise of joyful delights. Too many bars, and too much of that kind of attention had left her like a caricature of a windswept scarecrow. A human pole draped with rags.

"Ssssh!" Someone suddenly hissed. Nobody spoke nor breathed - they were always in an animal state of alertness. It was part of their nature, and now they were all poised for fight or flight, very rarely did they fight - but they were very adept fugitives. Red hoisted the crate Minny had been sitting on above the fire and set it silently over the flames. Not one spark escaped and immediately the dancing shadows of the group were gobbled up by the surrounding darkness. Footsteps and voices came from one of the maze of nearby alleys.

"S' them there guards so it is." Whinged a terrified Minny.

"Troubles for us. A told yis. A told yis." said Hunchy with mad glee.

"Time to scatter. Go wi' care y'all." Said Red. With some rustling and a scuffed foot or two, they slid perfectly into the night's gloom. Night was their natural camouflage, and they used it so very easily. There was an elegance about the ability of these uncouth ones to vanish so expertly. Just the way a flock of shimmering gulls disappear, as if by magic, into the sky's paleness on a spirally up-draught, so these ones slip just as easily and silently into the streets and alleys of the town around them.

<u>The Palace.</u>

The King was an angry man. He was also a small man, and plump, quite plump. None the less he was the King, all-powerful in his domain and with an ego far beyond his physical stature.

He stepped from his gold adorned bath, puddles of fragrant water formed on the marble floor around him. He smiled, just a little, for his mood was not good, as he watched the water flow into amoebic shapes on the polished stone. I like to leave a mark he thought. Wrapping a soft robe around himself, he walked into his bedchamber. The rage rumbling through him was growing; the bath had not really helped at all.

"I am going to make an example of that damn boy."

"Be cautious Highness." Advised Bishop Hautii, the city's leading churchman and the King's closest adviser. Hautii was lean of body. And even leaner of spirit - but clever, and very, very tricky. He had jumpy, conspiring eyes. "We don't want to stir up trouble. There are some that are happy, not many, but some. The rest will do as told, so long as they have a little something. And of course balance is important - it helps to keep them slightly more fearful than they are angry."

"Ner a one spoke - save that impertinent pup. The whole idea is to show them. All of them. From the richest to the most miserable that - I am in charge. No! Caution be damned, it's an example he'll be. And a bloody good one too. The next time I do that. Or anything. Anything! That takes my mind! In my own city - they'll applaud. Yes they'll applaud, and not a one will make a remark."

"Is it worth the risk Sire? Doing something like that again. Make an example of the brat then, but don't do that. Not like that. Not again. Think of your - mmm." Hautii's eyes were bouncing about in their sockets as he carefully composed his words. "Your constitution. If nothing else" The King carried on as if he had not heard the advice.

"I'll make that boy sorry. And I will clear the city of the likes of him. The people don't like them. There'll be few objections to that. Thieves and dirty parasites every one of them, always begging, and loitering, and pilfering. We'll rid the city of them, and everyone will be glad. Grateful subjects they'll be."

Hautii had not gotten to be powerful and influential by being slow. He knew when to speak, when to nudge or hint a little, or more usually when to flatter. But much, much more importantly he always knew when not to say a word. The King had his mind made up. Hautii knew he was not for turning. The royal blood in his veins was stubborn and vindictive. And of course stupid - the result of generations of in-breeding. But the sly bishop nodded as if agreeing with him totally. The King would have his revenge on the boy. And do whatever he wanted in his own city, he always did.

Already the night guards were beginning to arrest street people, blind or crippled, young or old, it mattered not.

<u>The Cell</u>

Scratcher had been with in the alley with Red and the others. When the alarm was raised, he had jumped a fence and found himself in a stable with some startled mules. The animals became agitated. Scratcher knew they would bring attention to him. He climbed onto the stable roof and then slid down into a different alley. As he hunkered behind a pile of stinking refuse he heard feet coming down the alley towards him. There was a darker slot in the surrounding darkness, quietly he slid into it. It was a deep doorway and he vanished into its welcoming blackness. No sooner was he flattened against the unseen door than figures rushed past. A torch of crackling pitch lit up the alley. They stopped near to where Scratcher was hiding. The newly arrived light was not yet a threat; it just made the doorway's shadow darker and more protecting.

Then it struck.

The punishing affliction which had given him his name. Suddenly it burned on his chest and down his legs. That was the way it always happened, one minute he was fine and the next he was being tortured. Scratcher had worked in the Royal lime quarry at one time. Hard work, poor pay. However the white stone demanded a price from those who toiled to hack it from the earth. Some it blinded, slowly burning their sight from them. Others it punished in lesser ways. It had left Scratcher with a skin that sometimes itched right down to his bones. He could not keep a job, too much scratching to be done at times. His skin was always covered in sores, some scarlet fresh and bleeding, others scabby and half healed.

The lime had put him on the streets. But at least nobody in the tribe of misfits to which he now belonged objected to Scratcher's need to tear at his skin. They did plenty of scratching themselves.

Well poor Scratcher could not leave the itching. He had to. Just had to. And so he tore at himself.

He might as well have shouted, "Here I am!"

And lo' he did not even get to satisfy his itch. At first he had tried to gently and quietly pat himself for relief. It was not enough; soon he was scraping violently through his clothes, at the hateful, demanding skin.

Flurries of baton blows send him to his knees. Scratcher blacked out. He awakened alone in a dank grey cell, no pristine white lime-washed walls here. Pain filled his body and the torture was still searing his skin. And now, with two broken arms he could not scratch.

The thick walls and the darkness soaked up his agonised cries as the rats sniffed and licked at his tasty scabs. It was not long before the rodents were greedily gorging themselves on his succulent sores. He might as well never have existed - and soon he wished himself dead.

The Bakery

Scratcher's friends had each returned to their boltholes. Tall, inhospitable church towers, dusty black coal cellars, tatty, and damp garden sheds, smelly stables, smellier sewer holes, disused workshops, even mouldy burial crypts. These places all provided regular shelter for the city's dispossessed. Each had their own favourite lair; here they hid a sleeping blanket, rolled around a few bits and pieces. Maybe relics of another life, or a useful tool, or something to sell when things got very bad. A life's petty treasures, sadly hidden in a thin, decrepit blanket – stashed in a place belonging to someone else.

On cold nights dozens of them spend the night sleeping behind the bushes by the bakery. Here the heat from the sweltering ovens filtered through the walls, helping ease the chill. On cold winter nights scraggy dogs, scraggy humans and scraggy cats, all jockeyed for the best positions. When it was really frosty they all pushed together into a stinky, heaving pile of life. Steamy breath rising from the writhing mass, hanging in the painful air like fumes coming from a ripe compost heap.

Though it was summer, Red headed to the bakery bushes this night. He was more sad and lonely than usual. It was here he had first met and befriended the boy with the long yellow hair, perpetually smiling face and a way of always, innocently, talking the truth. A cruel frost had glittered on everything that night, sparkling with a killing beauty. So the crowd of miserable beings all pushed tighter together than usual. Their breath mingled, gossamer veils floating in the marble light of the unkind, winter moon.

"Look mister. You're breathing my breath. We all do that you know. Breathe each others breath. It used to be in you and now it's in me" The boy had said as he shivered beside Red. And so the friendship began.

Red had once been a teacher. Yet he had learned so much from this boy. Most of what he learned were simple things, things he already knew, but had never really paid much attention to. Like how they, the street people, were no different from other people, it was just their situation which was different. Naive wisdom was how Red thought of it.

The fever that years ago had taken Red's wife and girls away forever had nearly taken his mind away, it had left for a long time, and sometimes he wished it had never returned. He remembered them, but did not really remember how he ended up on the street. It was home now, and felt right, a fitting penance for having survived. They had come to him that cold night when he had first met the boy. Laughing happily, loving him, gently touching his clean shaved cheek and hugging and kissing him and calling him daddy, and darling, like on so many other terrible nights. A horrible kaleidoscope of fractured memories, the same pieces repeated in so many different patterns - all ending in the nightmare of awakening to the truth. And he had cried into the cold night, and the boy had cried with him, and for him. He had not questioned why this youngster was not in a warm home with a protecting mother on such a freezing night. He had just sucked in the boy's proffered sympathy, used it, just as he used the free heat from the bakery, before falling back into an unhappy sleep. By morning the boy, like the cats and dogs, was gone. But the streets make a small world and soon they met again. They became the most unlikely pair of friends. The man was protective of the boy, and the boy allowed himself to be protected and parented - after a fashion.

Now on this night Red lay thinking of the boy's startled face as the King's guards had moved so quickly through the crowd, like wolves on a rabbit, they had caught and whisked him away in a flash. Finally Red fell into another tortured sleep, and the boy joined his wife and the girls. Beautiful, healthy, laughing faces – careless of woe, they mocked his wretched rest.

The Square.

Life in the city began to change. For the dispossessed, the world had been turned on its head. Scratcher was not the only familiar face to disappear. Beggars no longer jostled for the best spots. Street music fell silent. No one hustled for odd jobs around the shops. The whole population noticed the changes. Some said it was good, many others asked. "Who next?"

Eventually the boy was brought bound and confused to the main square. Red and a few companions watched from a rooftop. Crowds thronged the square around the platform where the scaffold and whipping post sat, a prominent and permanent threat to all. A guard read a very short proclamation. "This person has insulted the King, our Leader and Guide." He paused and arrogantly looked around the watching crowd before continuing. "Today he will die!"

At first only those standing closest to the platform heard. But the news spread on a hushed, murmuring wave. It spread throughout the square and across the city, to the rooftops, and all the other places where the boy's stunned companions were watching and hiding. Everyone, tramp and rich man, poor man and tradesman, every one of them - had expected a flogging that day. No one expected this.

It was over in a flash. Suddenly the boy was convulsing and jerking like some drunken puppeteer's marionette below the scaffold, - his yellow hair and open, cheerful face - covered with a rough canvas bag. There were several muted shouts of "Shame!"

However the people cleared the square quickly. They were shocked and frightened. And not one of them had any doubt about who was in charge.

Someone had knocked Red out. Several of them had jumped on him, but nobody was sure who had clonked him. It was the only way to restrain him and prevent him from leaping down and vainly charging to the scaffold. They managed to drag him over the city roofs to the temporary safety of an old and abandoned tannery.

<u>The Crypt.</u>

Things got worse. Everyday more of the city's unfortunates were lost from the streets. Red was unaware of what was happening. Skinny Minny plied him with stolen gin - to keep him from rushing off to a raging destruction. They were now holed up in an ancient crypt. Her, Red and Hunchy, and the boxed remains of the original tenants. Slowly he began to refuse the cheap liquor. It was a refuge he had been to before, and through his stupor he knew it was only an illusion of sanctuary. The boy was weeks dead when Red returned - sick and dreadful - to his awful world.

By then, the King's cull of the desolate was near complete. Somehow Hunchy had kept in touch with those few others at liberty. One night they all met in the crypt, hungry, afraid, and huddled together in their hopelessness. There were only nine of them left, and they were despondent. The King was to parade through the city the next day. The talk was that he would indulge in more arrogant nonsense. They hated him and his cruel pride.

"There is something we can do!" Red said slowly and deliberately to those around him in the miserable grave. An oily rag give them a dull, smoky light. They were seated on ornate coffins, roughly dragged from their crevices for the purpose. Some had been so old that they had shattered when moved, their bony contents rattling as they spilled onto the dusty floor. "We can do what the boy did. And maybe more. After all, we above all people have nothing to lose." At first they were frightened by what he proposed, but it dawned on each of them, he was right. They had nothing to lose. Even Hunchy agreed.

And so they spent the night, sitting amidst the scattered bones of their betters - discussing the crazy, desperate plan

<u>The Square</u>

Trumpets blared out gloriously; the sound resonated throughout the city, down the little streets, echoing across the squares, filtering into even the meanest alleys. The King strode out, accompanied by his flunkies, to parade through his assembled subjects. Again the population was astounded by his arrogance, but they did applaud, just as required.

Red and his band had positioned themselves in a narrow alley near the main square, close to the scaffold where the boy had died. The King approached slowly and deliberately, dripping with conceit as he savoured every moment of his power play. The insincere applause rippled along with him.

"Remember the boy. He died for speaking a harmless, simple truth. Remember the missing, before long we'll be a join' 'hem so we has nothing to lose, nothing to fear." Red encouraged his comrades.

The no-hopers had become a company of warriors - desperate and with their backs to the wall - they were about to go into battle.

And so they struck.

They leapt shrieking, with no weapons but their bodies and their desperation, into the path of the King's entourage. They shouted out as the boy had done. "Look. The King is naked."

But as they shrieked and screamed they tore their own clothes off. "Just like us. He is naked. We are all naked. We are all wrinkly and hairy and naked"

"Tiny, fat and naked." Screeched the nude Skinny Minny at the King.

And so the fool was.

Their ancient genitalia bounced, wobbled and quivered. Loose saggy skin, unwashed and unseen for years, was flaunted rebelliously.

Minnie's scrawny breasts swung with abandon. Spotty, hairy arses farted and were shook deliberately in the pink perfumed face of his astounded Regal Majesty. They danced and jumped madly in the square – but slowly, like a deadly plague, a blanketing silence descended over the awe-struck crowd. Like the frightened stillness which had accompanied the arrest of the boy. This huge quietness stopped their cavorting. No one moved, everyone was mesmerised by their madness, even themselves. People turned into statues, frozen in bewildered shock at the absurdity of it all.

Then someone in the crowd, either emboldened by the action of the paupers, or struck careless of his own fate by such a spectacle, yelled out. "So he is! The King is naked. He is naked! Just like the tramps and beggars."

And so this solitary shout was followed by several more.

Then a pounding tidal wave, a tumultuous noise, rose and washed the silence into oblivion. Shouts of derision and bellowing laughter filled the air, and the crowd heaved and surged towards the procession. By this time even the guards were laughing.

Hautti had cleverly moved away from the King, who was left standing naked and alone. He was like a little pink pig tethered to a post, petrified and helpless - watching the huge butcher approach with his knife. You would not listen, thought Hautii. You pompous fool. And he sniggered into his silken sleeve as he left the scene and headed to the comfort and security of his cathedral.

And so - this King lost power. And later someone made a song of the day.

"Bishops and burghers saw finery,
And wonderful,

silken hose.
But some of us
stood -
Where the boy had stood -
At the very edge of the crowd.
We saw naked lies -
And shouted out the truth –
Now unafraid –
Of the threat of a shroud."   *(m.j.c. – 1992)

Is this – The End?

FRIEND OR FOE?

" the only time I feel at ease is swinging up and down in the coconut trees"

Ray Davies

FRIEND OR FOE?

Jesus I was glad to lie here. On my back. On this small bank, puffing and sweltering. The sun had lost its will to punish and was now hanging low, but the day was still very hot. And I was tired, in spirit and in flesh. Sweat gushed from my every pore. Thankfully the high tech fabric of my shirt and pants quickly wicked it away from my skin. Except on my back, this was pressed hard onto the ground. My back was wet and warm. It was like a bed I had just peed in. Years ago - back in the home. But now I had a greater dread than matron in the morning, now life was worse than just miserable. It was – indescribable how awful this all was.

Pebbles pressed and pained my damp flesh but I cared little, in fact I was comforted by this pressure. I could feel pain and discomfort – that meant I was still alive.

It seemed as if the whole planet was lying just beneath me, and I was nothing but a lonely speck on its great big, curving surface. My hands were toying and rubbing the dry earth, digging into it - for grip in case I slipped off the planet and tumbled away into space. I was breaking little compacted pieces of the Earth into dust - using my thumb and fingers. These grains of silica and dirt were like the souls and desperate spirits of the people we had extinguished in our time here. People slipping into oblivion - or heaven - as easily as these grains of sand slipped through my fingers. Deep down inside me I wanted the earth to take me back, to embrace my bones, to let the sun warm my dust - and then to send it - spiralling, carefree - like the primeval stardust it was - without suffering before the wind.

What a release that would be, no consciousness, no feeling. I wanted to be scattered widely - so as to touch everything that was good in the world. To have my soul reassured that goodness and kindness still existed. Freedom. Free from the cruelty and barbarity which had encompassed me and had become ingrained over the past months.

My rifle lay across my chest - where it jumped a little with every beat of my heart. Most of the shooting had stopped. There were only occasional shots now, but between each sharp crack my gasping breath and thumping heart were the loudest sounds in my head. Because of the blitzing noise of the shoot-out my brain and my ears felt numb, as if they were no longer mine. My jumping rifle was covered in dust. And I remembered the constantly yelled mantra of a hateful drill instructor – A dirty weapon can get you killed -. Right now I did not care.

There is a comfort in not caring whether you live or die. The pressure of worrying about survival in battle is an immense burden. It is better to let the training and discipline they have inflicted upon you to take over. If you really cared then you would damn to hell their discipline, and the lost self you have become. And that will get you killed.

It is Heller's famous military Catch 22 - live to die, or die to be free.

The rifle felt more part of me than ever in this position, it rose and fell with every breath - as well as jumping with every heartbeat - it had become part of my life-force.

Yet I didn't even know if I had any rounds left in the mag.

Through my clotted senses I began to hear other sounds, men shouting to each other, the hissing voices of radio transmissions and the metallic clicking and clacking of guns being reloaded. God, more of this - then I let go and drifted into a daydream and as I did so I again briefly heard the hateful voice shouting at me – Always concentrate. Lack of concentration will get you killed – I still didn't care. I just kept drifting.

I was at the beach with two pretty girls, - and Tom, all four of us lying in the sun on warm sand.

The sky was a faultless blue, a couple of sun-gleamed seagulls drifted silently and effortlessly across my vision. I was carelessly playing with the sand, enjoying the feel of it - as I rubbed it between my fingers and thumb.

And I wanted to stay there. I no longer wanted to be absorbed by the earth. I just wanted to lie on this pleasant part of it. This was nice, just nice. Tom was saying something, his normal steady tone replaced with some sort of urgency

–Jesus I thought you were hit. Are you sleeping? Christ you are! You're f**king sleeping. Don't you know that can get you killed?

I reluctantly opened my eyes and turned my head to look at him. He looked like – well I suppose he looked to me as I looked to him. Same helmet, same uniform, same rifle, same hideous paint on the face, and now everything was brushed with the same dust. We all looked the same, in fact we all were the same, trained and honed and furnished for war. All doubt and independence removed. We weren't us - the guys any more, the bunch of trainee soldiers boozing and whoring our way through those few months – we now were us - The Unit. A single prowling animal, its savage instinct always bare and on show. I didn't speak; I just punched him, friendly like, on the shoulder. He was lying on his belly, his rifle snug into his shoulder and pointing over the over the stones of the tumbled wall we were sheltering behind. He was the best friend I had ever had. I was so glad I had met him.

I had joined the army for the comfort of it.

Since leaving the orphanage at 16 I had already been like dust on the wind, constantly blown into bad corners and crevices. Living here, working there, moving on, waiting for instructions - or a reprimand. A persistent stranger - on nodding terms with a few - and knowing nobody. And nobody knew me, which was a big hurt. The army would be like coming home to the only kind of life I really understood. A set time and way to do everything and somebody to tell you how and when - a why, was not really necessary. I would be wearing the army's clothes, eating their food, and living in their buildings. Just like the home; the only life I had ever really known.

Tom and I had met on our first day in the training base. He had been friendly, the sort of person who invites you into their sphere easily and confidently. Tom was the first person who had ever gotten to know me as an adult. When with Tom I felt no unease, wherever we were, no matter whom we were with. I could always draw on the sureness he had of his own space. I did not try to copy him or anything.

I just felt ok about me when I was with him.

God it's nice to feel ok about yourself. At the time you do not even think about it. It's later; when alone - that you realise how easy and natural it had been - then after a while the familiar doubt starts to creep back.

Tom and I went on leave together. We stayed with his family for a few days. I had never ever been with a family before; it was really great the way they had all made me feel welcome. I liked the way they talked to each other and even they way they shouted at each other. It wasn't like how people shout at each other in other places – it was nice shouting, like _ Tom are you going to be all day in the bathroom?- and the food was beautiful. Then him and I went to the beach for a week and had fun. Girls always seemed to like

Tom, he's not that handsome, but they laugh and joke with him. We had a blast of a time before heading back to the camp. Tom made me feel good, he had given me a hope I had never had - nor understood before.

And now here we were in a place without hope. In spite of all the equipment - and structure of command - and all the training and briefing - there really was no right or wrong - we just were an illusion of order and morality in this turmoil. This place sucked everyone and everything into a vortex of desolate hopelessness. Life had evolved into a selfish scramble to continue to exist; there was never a question about the collateral cost to innocents.

Will you look at this – said Tom – But stay low.

I did not want to move - but I turned over and, resorting to type, kept my head low and carefully looked out over the wall. As I did so I realised someone was crying out and moaning. I could not understand the jumble of words. It was one of the enemy, lying about 50 yards away, in helpless agony. The dust around him was muddy and black from the blood emptying out of his shattered leg. Some way beyond him one of his comrades had left the shelter of an ancient stone shed and was crawling forward to help him. A couple of burning vehicles were giving them some cover from the rest of our unit; the oily smoke billowing up and around them added further protection. Only Tom and I could see them clearly.

The rescuer was clearly aware of the danger he and his wounded comrade still faced, he moved slowly, hugging the ground like a lover. Someone else on our side must have been getting glimpses of him because occasional pot-shots coming through the smoke sent fountains of earth into the air close to him. The shooter was only seeing him through patches in the smoke and was obviously guessing at his position. But the rescuer was deliberately not crawling in a straight-line; he was zigzagging and going the long way to his injured friend.

He was a brave man.

Each time I heard a shot I began to hope it missed, and so far they all had. Soon I felt as if I was crawling with him. Like becoming totally involved in a soccer match, my legs began to move for him, as you do when you go to kick an imagined ball as you watch the match from afar.

I was holding my breath as I willed him on. I wanted the smoke to thicken and envelope them both, to hold them in its opaqueness until they were out of danger. Why was someone shooting at them still? They were not a danger: the rescuer did not even have a weapon – the only things he was carrying were love and courage.

Suddenly something about his movements changed. Had he been hit? Then I understood – he had just seen me and Tom. He was staring across at our position. He could have been one of us. The uniforms and the painted faces were nearly the same, and the dust was exactly the same. His eyes gleamed – clean and fearless from - the disguised mask of a face. I stared back – hard - trying to communicate my empathy; surely he could understand I was no threat. I was on his side; I wanted him to succeed in his act of love. He must have understood because he turned back to his mission, ignoring the danger we posed. Slowly he edged closer to his goal and eventually he got a grip on the collar of the casualty's jacket. Obviously exhausted he lay motionless for a while, the smoke had indeed thickened and the shooting had stopped. I imagined I could hear his breathing as he tried to regain his stamina for the crawl back to safety, I could still hear his companion groaning. Then he started squirming around to change direction and as he began to crawl back his friend screamed in pain at being hauled along in such a desperate way. More shots rang out in response to the pitiful cry. Luckily they only struck the ground again to throw more lumps of the earth leaping into the air. Neither of them had been hit but the screaming stopped and the rescuer fumbled with the victim. He must have been checking to see if he had died or had fallen unconscious. I thanked God to see him struggle on with the rescue. Their journey to safety was marked by a shiny trail of blood. It looked like engine oil spilled across the dirt.

A burst of automatic fire trailed the thick smoke into spectacular swirls as it whistled through it before splattering a pattern around them. Again I was thankful to see they were not hit, but someone was still determined to fire in blind hope of killing them both.

They were getting closer to the shed and the hands of less brave comrades began to appear, waving encouragement and urging the rescuer to greater effort. They wisely were not attempting to give them covering fire trough the smoke, this would surely have brought heavier return fire from our boys.

At last they were at the shed, just another two yards and they would be around the corner closest to us, and this would give them full cover from the fire they had been taking.

I realised I was still holding my breath as I suddenly inhaled greedily. Obviously Tom was as enthralled by this drama of life and death as I was because neither of us had spoken. I let my breath out again with a sigh of relief as they rounded the corner and the rescuer pushed himself up to lean against the stone wall. He put his head back and gulped air for a few seconds before pulling the wounded man's head and shoulders onto his lap - as a mother would do for a sick child.

I could see him talk down to him and stroke his head with a dirty hand.

It was an act of kindness and humanity such as I had never seen before.

Their comrades too must have been aware of us – and wary - because they were still only offering hand gestures as help.

They were not to know we too were willing their friends to safety. The rescuer's eyes flashed towards us – was he trying to thank us?

I glanced what I thought was a look of camaraderie back to him. His selfless action had been the greatest thing I had witnessed since coming out here. It did not matter at all that he was an enemy – or so I had been instructed to believe.

Crack! Crack! Two shots. Right by my ear - deafening.

The rescuer's chest was suddenly emblazoned with crimson as the wounded man's head exploded over him. Then he himself slid slowly down the wall, his own mess of a head drawing a bloody red arc down the dry stone as he too slipped into oblivion.

That surprised the f**kers – Laughed Tom. I screamed at him. Why? Why did you f**kin do that?

Why! I don't know f**kin why. I just did. What's wrong with you?

I could not believe what he had done.

I shot him.

-Right in the face.

There were rounds in the mag after all.

-Between the eyes.

I saw his horror, and the fear in those eyes - before they

disappeared in a red maelstrom of bone - and brain - and hair - out the back of his skull. Then I wept.

GOD'S HANDS

" when trouble gets too close to home - I turn the other way"

Christy Moore

GOD'S HANDS.

Ian's hand trembled ever so slightly. He registered this small emotional disturbance, but he did not hesitate. Steady again, and without another hint of feeling he cut.

The bright edge of the blade flashed like the facet on a diamond before disappearing into the woman's flesh - deep.

Her body was absolutely still now.

A slash of red oozed. Viscous. Bright with life giving oxygen - it trailed a string of vermillion pearls along the smiling wound of his cut. The ruddy pearls clung to the edge of her skin for a moment - before their surface tension failed – and then they ran, like scarlet ribbons, away from the from the rip in her body. The warm blood cooled quickly on the cool, white skin.

Her pale complexion was smooth and waxy. Beautiful. He thought she looked like Disney's Snow White, lying in motionless perfection in her crystal coffin. His hand had never, ever, trembled before. He knew this part no longer excited him, but the first time - when he had been exalted, his mood pitched high and expectant; even then his hand had been steady as a rock.

As his bloody hands automatically manipulated the blade his mind sourced the cause of the uncharacteristic tremor.

He had been thinking of the future. That was it. A future where a greater exaltation awaited. Fulfilment on a different plane. Ecstasy - beyond any drug - was to be his. The end of a great quest was nigh. Orgasmic-like pleasure palpated through him at the thought.

***

Obsession can make a beast of burden of a person. Ambition, lust, retribution, greed, evangelistic fervour, all can become yokes. Controlling direction, restricting movement to within the furrow, forever driving their beast on. Always becoming heavier, always restricting vision. Always demanding more. More time, more effort, more often. And always, always, - more fulfilment. Some people resist, they begin to see the forever unchanging road ahead. They do not know where their struggle against the burden will lead. Yet they struggle and eventually manage to throw off their yoke. And many find joy in this new freedom. Others are forever unaware of another way and become victims of their own constant obsession.

But not Ian. He was neither struggler nor victim.

He had created - and controlled this goal. Before he was an adult he had thought of it - had planted it firmly in his brain - and deep in his breast's core. From there it pounded through him, reaching into even the narrowest capillary with every blood pumping beat. Every second of every minute he knew it was there. He nurtured it. He lived for it. Worked hard for it - no wife could have had a more attentive husband. When he was young he was not sure how it would flower, just that it would. It was part of him.

Well the blossoming was now close. Oh, ever so close.

***

He felt his blood-soaked hands tremble again. He erased the future for the moment, and forced himself back to the present. Back to the task in hand.

The woman was young, and in spite of her pallor her good looks were obvious. They always seemed to be good-looking, and certainly wealthy.

Soon it was over. He felt nothing. Yet it used to satisfy him so much.

"Well that's that. She will be fine. Tony you finish. Sew her up and I'll see her tomorrow."

To reassure himself he took a last check at the 3D hologram of his patient's brain. The image was clear and precise, just like his work. Everything was perfect. He left the operating theatre - another miracle completed.

The whole team stared after him. This was the first time he had ever left before an operation was fully completed. Some of them had been with him for years - and he had never before done anything to surprise them. Ian was steady and predictable.

And a genius.

One of those people who shine as brilliantly as a flawless jewel.

But like most mortals Ian was like a pool of still water. We are all the same; the bright argent surface often only reflects the light coming from outside, constantly reacting to the environment around us – dispensing the niceties of life – a nod and an hello here, a smile and a meaningless conversation there. However all humans – bar the simple minded – are deep, darkly shadowed pools. A lurking mystery where tiny, unseen creations of the mind spring to life. Dim and bright, cabbalistic and open, benevolent and evil, they exist together in this pool of still water, some for a lifetime and some but fleetingly. We all experience these creations - thoughts and feelings which can sometimes make us uncomfortable with our own consciousness - these are things we would never dare share with anyone. They struggle for recognition. Devouring each other and re-birthing in new forms. Some disappear, like a popping bubble gone forever, others settle into the sediment below. Into the underworld of the mind. A different layer. Deeper - harder to probe. The scraps from above are refined here by other ferocious mind-beasts - to be filed somewhere in this enveloping dark trench of the being. This is the nearly unfathomable sub-conscious. And so the struggle continues - until almost everything is processed down to a smooth oneness. A manageable mess of mind and soul. And so we learn to live with ourselves – but this can be the most difficult relationship many people ever have.

The surface is yin, throwing the light back inoffensively. But this, this is yang – deep, disturbing, and darkly private. Another dimension - as binding and crushing as a cosmic black hole. Controlled chaos - awaiting a big bang - which thankfully in most cases is never triggered

With most people occasional shafts of light play through to their depths, sometimes alarming and disturbing these observers of their own souls, but in turn granting restraint a chance. These shafts of lucidness allow most of us to live as normal, non-threatening individuals, dealing with our hurts, grievances and disappointments. Then there are others who are never aware of anything but their bright, reflective surface. Ignorant to their darkness beneath, until sometimes suddenly - and without warning - something sets off the big bang. It crashes from below. Exploding into bedlam through the calm surface. Like a giant whale launching itself from the silent sea at the starry heavens in a maelstrom of noise and movement. And in that one maniacal moment they can destroy forever the world they have known.

But not Ian, he was neither of these. He never got a quick glimpse of his darkness. Neither was he ignorant of it.

Because he never forgot his darkness. His darkness comforted him. And it drove him; he kept it securely locked under the polished surface, vacuum-sealed beneath the flawless lid. But he was always in control.

Observers only saw the serious, yet boyishly handsome face, topped with a curly rush of fair hair, now silvering around his ears, and pale skin brought to life by the flashing radiance of jade eyes. Eyes brimming with life, searching and always computing, yet able to flash warmth and charm in a blink. These eyes and face were known the world over.

No other neurosurgeon in the world could do what he had just done. He was as famous as any film star, sportsman, or politician. He was constantly in the spotlight. The world's most eligible bachelor. No one knew he was already married; to the thrusting drive of his own subterranean emotions.

Ian was the most famous doctor since Christian Barnard. Though he tried to shun the press - they pursued him. From the time of the first facial transplant he had never been out of the headlines. They married him off, speculated on his sexuality, and tried to anticipate his research. In return he despised their patronising adulation, their shifting sand-dune like opinions, and most of all their shabby, lowest common denominator morality.

Ian now carried out life changing operations routinely. The world's best surgeons joined him to learn his techniques. Like an evangelist he was happy to teach those who would listen. And like a messiah he had so much to teach. Full facial transplants. The first full optic nerve transplant. A surgical cure for Alzheimer's and Motor Neurone Disease. Then total reversal of trauma-induced paralysis - and now speculation was mounting that this Noble Laureate was about to cross a new threshold. A journey beyond the flight of Icarus, a leap beyond Neil Armstrong's small lunar step. He was about to fly in the Sun God's face; by challenging the limits of human existence.

Ian's research had convinced him the brain could live for hundreds of years. Unlike the heart and other organs it did not wear out. Nothing physical to do, no endless pumping or filtering, no pollutants to choke it. It just sat there in its own specially evolved environment, facilitating minute electrical impulses and housing that which we would never understand fully – the mind - what some call the soul. The brain really was the temple of all good and all evil.

It was in here that every man's spirit dwelt. All the evil the world had ever seen had been spawned in a human brain. And all any brain needed was a new support system - every few decades to keep supplying the proper nutrients and stimuli. It was simple really. Keep the brain and dispose of the old, worn out body. Use total-body donors. A suitable enough solution in a totally throwaway society.

A full human brain transplant.

Medical Sci-Fi was how one journalist described it; another had called it a medical horror story on a Frankensteinesque scale. The social and moral debate which had surrounded Ian's full facial transplants was nothing compared to the outpouring of soul-searching perplexity this news was causing.

Throughout the world those with nothing better to do - and those who thought they knew better than everyone else - were marching and protesting about this "monstrous travesty of God's law".

Ian cared little about such things. He closed the lid firmly on such thoughts, leaving them to sink into the silt of oblivion. For him it was just the next step, another technical challenge.

***

Ian barely remembered his father. He too had been a genius - the man who had developed organic computers. Machines build around artificial proteins; they could make new internal links, upgrade and evolve naturally, and repair when required. Ian tinkered inside skulls in the same way his father had tinkered inside servers. To Ian it was all science, no ifs or buts, no qualms - just science. And science was the new religion. He found it hard to believe that at one time medical pioneers had had to sneak into back alleys - to secretly buy partially rotted cadavers - from desperate, drink-numbed grave robbers. Ian had no doubts about where he was going, others could worry all they wanted about the moral consequences of advancement. Pioneers could not afford to be watching behind - it was the way ahead which needed all their attention.

He had a gift and he had a mission.

Some said his genius was God given, Ian did not care - it was just his vehicle. God may have given him saviour hands - but the devil had given him drive; and a dark, consuming desire. Without these elements none of his miraculous accomplishments would have been possible. Only he knew that.

***

It was raining as he left the theatre wing and crossed to the research labs.

He looked up at the towering glass monument to wealth and power – the world's first mile high building - which dominated the complex. This was "the Corporation's" headquarters. The Corporation – officially called The J.C. Company - was the richest and most powerful organisation in the world and known worldwide just as The Corporation. The tower was also the home of the man who owned The Corporation, the same person who had made Ian's work possible. Briefly he thought of him, alone up there in his tower as he himself ran to get out of the rain. Security waved him through.

The caged apes were fairly quiet tonight. One or two seemed to grunt in his direction. If they did recognise him it was as a torturer, nothing else. He controlled their lives and their deaths. Some of them were now on their third brains. Earlier there had been problems - constant fits, no limb control, self-harm, and coma - but now there were no problems at all.

That was why he was now ready for the next step.

Through more security and he entered the lift and descended to the donor level.

Here the air is hushed and cool. The light is soft and bluish - like a summer dawn just before sunrise. It came from a battery of body capsules. The support machines hum and hiss quietly, a constant lyrical drone in the background, keeping the donor bodies fresh.

The Corporation had provided the people here. They were all young and had been fit before their sudden deaths. A suicide here, a drowning there, even some murder victims. They were all perfect for his research. Ian sometimes thought they were maybe just too perfect, but he never questioned their provenance.

Some people live and some people die - by fair means or foul. Like the early medical pioneers Ian did not care, the dead were really just a resource. Without them he could never have come this far in his accomplishments.

The Corporation owned the research institute; they owned the university, and the hospital. In some way they owned the people who worked and studied there. They thought they owned him too, Ian was aware of that – but he knew different.

***

The Corporation itself was owned and controlled by Jake Cooney – the J.C. for whom the company was named. His wealth and power were envied in every capital in the world, even in the Washington White House. He had just been speaking to the President of the European Federation and would shortly speak to the Chairman of The Federal Republic of African States. A massive trade- war was developing between the two blocks. Jake had still not decided if such an event would be good or bad for his Corporation. If Jake thought it were to be disadvantageous it would not happen. He glided quietly to the window in his wheelchair to ponder the situation.

It was raining on the city which lay glimmering before him.

When he looked down from here he often thought of the Devil tempting Christ in the desert - with the world's shining cities of sin. The reviled one had spread the world's riches before the worshipped one, and offered them to him. Well from here Jake could see a lot of what he either owned, or could buy easily - but he still was not sure if he was God or the Devil. Certainly he often believed he was nearly as powerful as either. He had enriched many lives when it suited him. Countless others he had left destroyed, causalities of his total pursuit of wealth and power. The streaming rain washed the city lights into refracted patterns on the glass. This was how Jake always saw the world, a fractured, disordered place awaiting his version of order. The weather was one thing Jake did not control yet. But it was being worked on.

High in this office in the sky he felt cocooned; the wet night intensified this comfortable feeling. A long time ago he had stopped experiencing any sense of loneliness. His isolation fed his feeling of power, the more alone he was the more potent the power felt - concentrated as it was solely within him. He did at times feel like the mighty Zeus, controlling so much from his lofty glass and steel Olympus. Jake certainly had God like ambitions.

This difficulty between Europe and Africa required some major decisions. This could be the biggest opportunity for the Corporation since Jake had allowed the Indian Subcontinent to be partially destroyed by Pakistan and India in the nuclear war of 2018. That had worked out well for the Corporation, giving it, and of course him enormous political power in Asia. Power he had consolidated throughout the world in the years since.

But Jake was a different man now. He was old and his feeble body, immobile and pain-wracked, now preoccupied his brilliant mind more than any other matter. The goblin like old man in the gliding chair resented, more and more everyday this base intrusion, of what he considered to be the ills of ordinary men, into the ever - calculating consciousness he had always been. However, like the weather, this too was being worked on. And he had confidence his prize- winning doctor would soon offer him radical salvation.

Jake liked Ian. He liked his unsurpassed talents and skill, his single-mindeness, his drive and desire. These were traits they shared. It was nearly 20 years now since Jake at last agreed to meet the young doctor who had been persistently trying every avenue to speak to him. And Ian had certainly been persistent, even sleeping on the street outside Jake's home for a week in his determination to see him. Yes, Jake had liked Ian straight away. And in the short interview he had been granted Ian had sold Jake his dreams and had been granted the resources for his revolutionary research. Jake was able to write off the research costs to tax. And the Corporation, spreading into other areas from its roots as an innovative I.T. company, received the plaudits for assisting such far-reaching medical research. Back then who could have imagined such glorious and far-reaching success for the Corporation - and the young doctor? And now Jake was on the brink of humanity's dream. Another chance.

Ian was going to give him a new life. Once again Jake would be young and strong, with a body fit to house what he considered to be the surest and most able mind in the world. And he had plans; the world would never forget Jake Cooney. He was now going to have at least one more lifetime to stamp even more of his influence on the world and its affairs.

***

When the big day arrived Ian was, uncharacteristically, a little nervous; but even so his hand was steady as a rock. The operation he had lived most of his adult life for was nearly over. The intense planning and timing of the past months had been worth it. The whole team was involved, split into three groups working in interconnecting theatres. Everyone had been surprised when Ian changed the plans to include a third procedure. He had suggested it late but was insistent about involving the ape.

He said he wanted to put the donor's dead brain into the ape. It would help in further research he had said. They knew Ian was right about it helping the research, but the senior team members felt a triple operation was stretching their resources too much. However Ian said he was confident he could repair the damaged brain and possibly, "re-facilitate its use."

The donor was perfect. Jake had come down to the donor preservation unit and chosen him himself. Strong and handsome, and such a clean death. A gang killing in Naples apparently, murdered with a stiletto straight through the base of the skull. Practically painless and bloodless. Such a lucky find Jake had said, almost ironically.

Ian did not think for a moment it had been lucky, but he cared little.

He moved quickly between the three theatres. Jake in one, the ape in one, and the handsome young cadaver in the third.

Ian was like a moviemaker, adjusting a set here, changing the script there, constantly directing and arranging his masterpiece. He was cool and collected as usual as he pushed the brain transfer modules between the theatres. Only he handled and removed and transplanted the precious organs. That was the protocol. The lasers fired on his command – cutting – repairing - sealing. The senior surgeons assisted with sewing and connecting of blood vessels and major nerves - but it was always Ian who made all the decisions – always Ian who directed. Without a doubt this was Ian's show - they respected and trusted him - implicitly.

Then without warning – devastation.

Ian hesitated for some reason – and the unbelievable happened - he panicked.

Alarms began to flash and bleep on all the systems. First the donor, now with Jake's wonderful brain in place began to flat line. Ian seemed to go to pieces. Confusion reigned. They tried to restore order. To no avail. Ian was the only one who could possibly have retrieved the situation – but he appeared to be in shock.

The new, dark and good-looking Jake died.

Jake's former body died. Only the ape survived, with the dead Italian's brain. It was a disaster.

The press had a field day; it was obvious they had been waiting on this.

The left-wing press said if he had succeeded only the rich would have benefited from such a radical procedure. They were right of course.

The right-wing press said God had struck the accursed project down. They were wrong of course.

Ian went to ground on the Corporation's private island in the Caribbean - well protected by its own formidable security force.

He was still there when Jake's will was made public declaring Ian to be his sole heir. There was disquiet in many quarters about the circumstances surrounding this will. Because it was made just before the operation. Little attention was paid to the fact that will making was a normal precaution before any major operation. And Jake himself had insisted upon it.

Those close to, no not close to, because he was close to no-one – those around Ian at this time noticed he had no interest in this revelation about the will. He did not seem to be depressed, nor terribly unhappy, about his failure, he was just different. One month later the failed operation and the scandalous outcome of the will were still news. Ian however announced he was going back to work. And he did.

He knew the technicians were watching him as for the first time he returned to the labs. But he did not care, he seemed happy as he approached the only survivor of that fateful day.

The chimp had been on a heart and lung machine since the operation. Ian had left strict instructions that no-one was to go near the dead beast until he returned. He started into his work.

For hours he worked by himself – still there hours after everyone else had left.

Only when he was sure he was absolutely alone did he do what seemed impossible – he roused the seemingly dead animal.

The ape began to come awake. Ian removed him from the support system and put him in a cage. It was confused. If anyone had been there they would have wondered how he had brought this animal, with its dead human brain, quickly back into a conscious state.

After a few hours as the groggy chimp began to adjust to its new situation. Ian approached the cage.

He took a yellowed piece of paper from his pocket; it was over thirty years old and Ian had carried since he was a boy.

It was a note from his father. A suicide note. It explained his father's death - and it had motivated and guided Ian's life.

In it his father accused his business partner of framing him for a murder so as to get total control of their growing company. His father died a death of shame, alone in his cell, despised as a cowardly killer. Ian cried as he held the note up before the monkey. The ape's eyes could see the note.

It was Jake Cooney who was named there as the betrayer.

And it was Jake's brain, trapped inside the monkey, which could understand it.

The monkey screamed and shrieked, he threw himself against the bars of the cage, blood gushed from many cuts as he hit the bars again - and again. Eventually the screaming monkey collapsed with exhaustion. It whimpered as it lay bleeding and partly conscious on the stainless steel floor of the cage. Ian sedated it again. He intended to keep doing this for a long time to come. To arouse it - and torture it - with the reality of its new existence in this specially created hell. If he wanted to Ian could keep doing this for decades.

God's hands had easily done the devil's work.

THE BEDROOM

"whatever gets you through the night - it's all right"

John Lennon

THE BEDROOM.

The curtain dimmed bedroom was still and peaceful - like a convent chapel. The silence was nearly joyful, but there would be no joy in this room again - not for us.

This was her room. I had always just called it the bedroom - she had always called it her bedroom, as in "Be nice to me or I might not allow you into my bedroom tonight". She often called it the heart of the family because, "this is where we made them all".

Together we had over the years changed it to suit our tastes and needs for a particular time. But it was definitely her room. She had more drawers, and more wardrobe space than me, and she had nearly all the surface space. Me - I was just happy to share it with her. I would have shared anything to be with her.

She had bewitched me when she was just sixteen, casting her spell naturally and innocently - just by being her, no pretend coyness, nor awkward teenage flirting – she was just so pretty and so nice. And I had remained gladly spellbound for every one of the forty years since. No matter about all our ups and downs - that spell never broke. Her being the mother of my four children never stopped her from just being - my girl.

In my mind's eye she would always be a sixteen year old beauty with plaits.

Now as I sadly gazed down on her asleep it looked as if the big bed was starting to devour her. It was all fluffy-white and plump - and she had grown so tiny and thin. My dying little angel was now helplessly captured by her own betraying body - in the bed's cloudlike folds.

***

God - we had some times here - scarlet fun-filled nights. Candles in red glass. Exotic nights. Entwined shadows, huge and flickering on the patterned walls - so alive, so bold. Musky perfume. Dark music. The room had throbbed with heightened senses and expectations. Our own Hellfire Club – here - in the bedroom. For a few hours we would be the pulsating, absolute centre of our own universe. No thought of work, or children, or the exploding, life threatening Belfast streets. This room was a retreat, a haven – no, it was more than that. It was a kingdom. That's what we had done, we had built a kingdom in this house, the kingdom of our life together, and this room was its epicentre- the throne room.

What I wouldn't give for one more of those nights. For our kingdom back again. To worship my queen.

Our wonderful normality was now being cruelly extracted from us - through her. Cell by dying cell - layer by fading layer. Each day more of her life escaped through the pale translucent skin. Her gleaming emerald eyes were now like beach glass. Though a hint of the colour was still there beneath the frosted surface their mischief and sparkling promise was gone - forever. We were losing our kingdom with every small breath she managed to steal from the begrudging air.

Why? Why us?

Oh! Thundering anger here you come again. Rumbling through me. Shaking my legs. Twisting the muscles in my neck until they curl pain, like a breaking wave, right across my head. I chased it away; today there must be no anger. I had learned to control this resentful anger now - because I did not have the time for it. I had had important tending and loving to do these past months.

My panic was different from my flashes of anger. Though I also managed to I keep it in check it had been constant for all these months. Minute after minute it cracked and growled within me. Like pack ice – it was constantly shoving and moving, yet going nowhere - waiting for a destructive thaw which would be its only release. The pandemonium wanted to burst through and find release. Our world was disappearing and I had no response. Defeat was imminent. And I was powerless, hopelessly powerless. But in front of her I had kept the panic and the anger hidden. That is what we all do in a situation like this. We try, with a veneer of a smile and a feeble light-heartedness to plead ignorance to the awful truth, making a show of normality – for their sake – the sufferer, the victim, the soon to be dead loved one. And all this pretence is useless, for they know, only too well, the deadly inevitable truth. Because it has been mercilessly thrust upon them. Deep into their very being. It has invaded and become part of the essence of who they now are – their death was conceived at this truth's birth, and now - like two deadly twins they are bound together - in a journey to joint oblivion.

***

Her little breaths murmured a mantra into the peacefulness of the room; they were like a little pulse just below the silence. Their rhythm and the afternoon light, soft and embracing through the curtains gently drew me to her. I lay down on top of the covers beside her and held her waning little hand.

We were always one in this small space.

I stared, as if in a trance, at the white ceiling and then drifted through it to some distant, thought chasing nothingness.

My love, my love, where are you going?

What about us?

What about me?

Christ, what about me? A huge, expansive void was about to fill this small space. I knew it was going to crush me, like starlight sucked into a black hole. And the ensuing darkness would be forever. There would never be light in my life again.

She would call me selfish for these selfish thoughts. She used to call me selfish on weekend mornings because I would yell at the four kids to go into their own rooms and leave us to sleep. The echoes of their young voices and those boisterous attacks on our bed, leading to mass family tickling fights, would forever be part of our history in this room. Like the layers of wallpaper on the wall behind the wardrobe. I had always left a patch of the old paper there, under each new pattern - a hidden archive of our time here. I know that one day some stranger will surely steam and scrape it thoughtlessly away. Like us it will disappear.

***

They had all been weaned in this room. In a Moses basket that always sat at my side of the bed. Sleepless nights and teething gel. Bottle warmers, nappy pins, the smell of baby sick and talcum powder – all the consequence of too many red-perfumed nights. An uninvited little smile came with that thought. Although she was lying here beside me, and I was holding her hand - it was the loneliest smile in the world.

As they got older they were nursed here when sick, or sheltered between us from bad dreams. If I was half asleep I just hooked out an arm when one of them appeared at my head and scooped them up and over and down into the warmth between us. Like an old steam express grabbing a hung mailbag from the trackside and throwing it safely into the guard's carriage.

The twins had been born here - in this very room. That was a night. She thought it was cramps at first because she was not due until the following week. They came so easy. Just two strangers - slipping from the unknown - into our lives. When we realised they were on their way I called an ambulance, but they were crying with hunger on the bed, wrapped in two big towels, their cords still attached, by the time it arrived. The other two were hopping about between their room and ours as it was happening. Excited and scared, they giggled and hushed, and then giggled again as things unfolded. I was terrified, but she was calm and motherly through it all, calling out to the gigglers "Don't worry Daddy knows what he's doing." And winked at me with those luscious, teasing green eyes.

"This is your fault you know. You should leave me alone at night." She breathlessly laughed as she rode another contraction. She was always good with pain.

Now they were all off - building their own kingdoms. Their lives now grey and darkened by her illness. Today's plan had been emotionally disclosed to them – there was little discussion however. They all objected - saying the views of all the family had to be listened to, that we had to hope and pray for a miracle She was not strong enough to argue that she had lost all hope, that she could no longer go on, so I just put my arm around her and explained that in this situation we were a family of two. This was our business - like planning a family - this was just between her and me. They knew I was talking for her - and with a heart more broken than theirs. Their love for us both filled the room as they quietly accepted the inevitability of what was to come – we all cried gently together – as only a family can do at a time like this.

It had just been the two of us there when the doctor told us how sick she would become - and that nothing could be done for her. We came home and we lay for hours on this bed. Shocked, our thoughts churned in isolated silence. So close, yet barely touching each other. Part of me wanted to blame her for this affliction on our lives. She had brought this into our lives not me. My anger wanted to blame somebody, but of course how could I blame her. There was nobody to blame. And that only made it worse, this heartbreaking waste. No one had sent this as a judgement, a punishment – it was cruel fate – bad luck. So we just lay there – numbed. It was as if we had had a row. Like one of those times when a bed seems as wide as an ocean and two people lie - like immovable continents – a storm raging on the cotton sea between them.

That day drifted slowly away and the room became dark and cold.

So we got up and ate. We then tried to talk as we stared across the table at each other, but each time we tried one of us would start to weep. We drank wine, and smoked an old, dried up joint I knew had been lurking for a long time in the corner of a drawer. That night we fumbled a failed passion as we searched for an anchor - for the old secure reality - it had always been our safest retreat. God, we thought it would go on forever.

But now we had a new and broken world to deal with - nothing would ever be the same again.

I could have died for her the first time she soiled the bed. Her pain was burden enough, but this I knew was her big cross. The complete unpleasantness of it was deeply alien and shocking to her. She did not look at me as I cleaned the bed and her up. "Don't worry.

This is easy. I can do this my love". I told her, my words awash with all the compassion and love I felt for her in that moment.

She did not lift her head from where it fallen onto her raised knees, her arms clasping her legs and her hair hanging limply down over them as she replied "I cannot". Her voice was flat and beaten – yet her words were certain.

Those two words went to my heart like a dagger. I knew what they meant.

She could not speak to me, nor look at me for another two days, such was the shame she felt at her helplessness.

It was inevitable what was to follow.

***

Many times in the past we had sat and discussed the meaning of life - and death - and sin - and God. Easy discussions with a glass of wine in your hand, and a smug faith in your own continuing good fortune.

I was not sure about God – she was sure, she believed. In spite of this I was not sure about taking life, even early abortion – but she could see justified occasions for all such drastic and controversial acts. We would end these abstract discussions casually – each of us sure of our own position - and comfortable in the knowledge we would surely never have these positions tested. Poor human fools.

One night as I propped the pillows behind her for her to sit up and take some medicine, she affectionately stroked my face - and beginning to cry she said. "You love me – deeply. Into your very bones. I know this, deep into my bones. And I know you believe in hope. But I cannot. I cannot hope when I hurt like I do - and it is getting worse. I cannot hope when I know what I know. I cannot hope as I feel myself fading away. I cannot hope when you have to clean me like a baby. There is no hope my love. It will be over within months. But I cannot endure this all for months. Please, please, love me well - and release me from all this. Please". She had said it. I knew it was coming.

Then my poor love cradled my head in those sick, skinny arms as I sobbed - hopelessly into her impoverished hair. She knew I could not refuse her. Later as I battled my despairing mind I tortured myself with the thought she was being selfish by asking for this, after all, she knew I would not refuse her.

But really I knew she was desperate and had no where else to turn. In the end this was not about the kids, it was not about society or the moral judgements of others. This was about our life, the one we had made, the life that we owned together, unlike the drawer space in this room this one life was built on the total equality of our relationship, on our love and our respect for each other.

Only God - or one of us could end it.

And I believed both her and I had more rights here than God.

***

And so now, throughout this morning, I had fed her medicine and tablets, lots of tablets. She asked for some wine, why not we thought. But not too much in case she became so sick as to bring the tablets back up – that would complicate everything. God, we were being so scientific and practical. She smiled a lot, and we touched a lot. We whispered our love to each other, and talked of how we had met, and how lucky we were to have had this time given to us out of the infinite eternity of existence, and how wonderful our children were. I held and stroked her, continuing to gently talk to her as at last she fell into this, her most untroubled sleep for such a long time. I knew we would never speak again – Jesus this cannot be real, this is just not happening. But it was. This was happening to us. How can we never speak again? How can this be?

Oh! God! Help us. Help me.

I set her hand back down on the soft quilt and turned to look at her. She was breathing so softly, wherever she was now she was certainly not in pain. I had not seen her look so peaceful for months, and the loveliness of her face was there, delicately taut over her jaw and cheek bones and even a little colour in her cheeks – red wine always did that to her, flaming her face, she hated it when that happened. I knew I could not let her come back - I loved her too much. I could not let her down. She knew she could always rely on me and that I would never fail her. I cupped her head in my hands and kissed her lips – they felt cool – but as soft and yielding as ever, even now a flare of our passion briefly came over me. Judas.

He too had sealed his betrayal with a kiss. But no this was not a betrayal – this was her wish. Perhaps it had been Jesus's wish also? Was I Judas?

I felt more like a God as I clasped my pillow to my chest and rolled onto her.

I pressed the pillow, as gently as I could, over the face I had loved all my adult life.

Suddenly in the midst of this horror I remembered a day in 1972 - we had been caught up in one of those impromptu Belfast gun battles. The IRA at one corner, the British Army at the other, and us caught in the middle. I had pushed her to the ground and lay right over her as the bullets screamed above and around us. I did not heed her words. "You're smothering me. I can't breath" as I pressed her closer into the ground. I would have taken every bullet that came down the street just so I could protect her.

And now I was smothering her again.

My body was shaking. I felt her going. Her soul passed through me.

Touching every cell in my body. Into and right through my trembling heart - tearing it asunder - and out into the ether, to the unknown. Leaving me forever. I screamed a long anguished cry into the cold, empty room.

The room in which we had conceived and birthed life. Now together we had ended life here. Our throne room was now a bitter and sour place - desecrated. Some time later I rolled off her.

I took her small lifeless hand and held it tight.

I stared through the ceiling into nothingness. I cared for nothing. I was nothing.

The day drifted slowly out of the room - and it and my darling became cold.

A LITTLE BOY

" don't just lie there –it's a waste of your opportunities"
R. Ó Seachnasaigh.

A LITTLE BOY.

The sky was high and bright.

Beautiful.

Azure at the zenith, falling to ice blue at the shimmering horizons.

***

Nobuo smiled to the glorious morning as he watched his little boy play on his chrome trike –glittering and carefree –

in their garden on the edge of the city.

The plane's engines thundered as it sped through this glorious morning, its course traced – briefly –

by a glittering trail of ice crystals upon the blue dome.

Shinichi was his only son and sometimes Nobuo's heart thundered; such was the love and joy the infant brought him.

God, - Tibbits loved his plane; so much he had joyfully named it after his mother.

The child's eyes gleamed the sky's blueness up at Nobuo - their mahogany hue masked by the reflected heavens.

With pride Tibbits looked along the polished wing - where the heavens gleamed on the trembling silver.

Nobuo visualised a universe behind his son's eyes - as vast and wondrous as the one behind the sky.

And his heart was gladdened by the innocent love shining out at him.

Tibbits felt like Zeus, powerful and aloof - viewing the smallness of the earth from his riveted Olympus - as he mightily conquered the sky.

Such power gladdened his heart.

The past and the future lay in those eyes - the soul of his own mother, the souls of countless ancestors -

and the wonders his son would encounter as his life unfolded.

Tibbits wondered - was there was a Hades below the curving horizon – and would he be filling it this morning - with countless Japanese souls.

Nobuo's heart shook with the emotion of this lovely morning in the garden - with the love he shared with his wondrous little boy.

- Oh! The joy of it!

Tibbits's heart shook with pride because behind him - in the dark belly of his argent beast - lay a sibling, a wondrous Little Boy.

- Oh! The joy of it!

Enola Gay was about to deliver. Again it would be - another brilliant sun.

***

Shinichi became a singed and screaming blister.

Horrible.

Nobuo's heart thundered - as he buried him in their Hiroshima.

***

Author's Note:.

To this day the twisted metal that is now Shinichi's trike is on display in Hiroshima's Peace Park Museum.

Tibbits is regarded as an American hero. He said he never regretted his flight to Hiroshima.

FOOK!

"it's a job, grass grows, birds fly,
waves pound the sand. i beat people up"
Muhammad Ali

FOOK![1]

"Fook! I'm nervous as fook Dee."

"It'll be sound ar kid. Don't worry. I know what im doin. And stop the cursin – no need for that. Know ata mean."

"Sorry Dee".

"Settle yerself and just act normal."

"OK."

They walked on down the road without any more talking. It was just after nine a.m. and the traffic was crawling along beside them. People going to work, or to school – or whatever. Normal people shuffling along, doing normal things – well as normal as possible in Belfast in 1972. Dee and his young companion were about something different.

"Down here." Said Dee, and they turned into a street of terraced red brick houses. Each had a small plot in front – just about as big as a grave. They were both "involved" – that is they were members of a paramilitary group. Part of the growing conflict in Belfast and the rest of the island of Ireland. There were a few cars parked outside some of the houses. Mostly rust buckets.

"Number 12." Continued Dee.

He knocked the door. Confidently - as if he lived there.

---

1 Fook is a safe substitute for a common swear word – use whichever you are comfortable with.

" R' ya all right Dee?" Said the guy with long blond hair who answered the door.

"You need a haircut Whitey - an I'm sound, thanks for asking– this heres wee Desy." Dee said, nodding his head to indicate wee Desy as they went inside.

"Fook. You're a geg Dee. Ya say that every time ya see me. All right wee Desy". Whitey nodded. Then added in case wee Desi wasn't keeping up with events.

"I'm Whitey."

"Well every time I see ya still need a haircut." Dee said.

"Style Dee. Style." Said Whitey, patting his long locks lovingly.

"Aye all right - cheat-the-barber. Well what's the craic here then?"

"The house is ma uncle's and he's sound as a pound. He's away to work from early on.

I stayed here last night and the boys from across the town dropped the first part of the mix off. It's in the backyard – ".

"For Christ's sake Whitey - it was rainin last night. It'll be ruined, you're gona get yourself kneecapped."

"Wise up Dee. Do ya think I'm daft? I covered it up wi an ou bit a carpet."

"I hope its bloody good carpet. Let's have a luk at it."

The yard was fairly tidy. An old tin bath and a bike frame hung in rusted companionship beside each other on one wall. The wall was shedding its ancient whitewash which lay in curling flakes on the concrete yard floor. Against another wall there was a pile of wet and glistening coal. A lidded metal rubbish bin sat beside a wooden door in the last wall leading to the entry; which ran the length of the terrace of houses. The bin was pretty full and the lid was balanced on a pile of cinders and potatoes peels rising in a mound out of it. Leaned against it a soggy carpet of anonymous colour was carelessly tucked around a paper sack. Hi-growth Fertiliser – 56lb. Economy Bag was stamped in red onto the white bag. Dee pulled the carpet off and examined the unopened bag.

"Shite. It's damp Whitey ya eejit. Let's get it inta the house."

"Inta the house?" said Whitey.

"Aye. Ya shouda had it in last night."

"Nobody told me it had to come inta the house."

"I suppose we sorta thought you'da figured that out when ya saw the flippin rain. Did ya not get shown all this when ya were training."

"Naw I only gotta a couple of gun lectures. Never got trained on smokies."

"Jasus. Have I to showya what ta do? What about you wee Desi? Do you know anything about smokies?"

"Well I know a wee bit about puttin the detonators into the fuse - an all that."

"Puttin the bloody det in – an all bloody that. Are you two pullin my chain? Waita the Countryman hears this."

"What countryman Dee?" Asked Whitey

"Not what countryman. Thee Countryman. The guy who's bringin in the det, the fuse and the jelly – an all bloody that. The man who's goin make sure our damn bomb goes with a bang."

"Frig – I thought we were goin do it all ourselves. I was lukin forward to it. I even brought a pencil." Said wee Desi with a loud tut.

"Why? Were ya goin draw it?" Laughed Whitey.

"Naawh. Ya use a pencil ta put a hole in the gelignite. Then you stick the det inta the jelly - after you've crimped the fuse inta the det. Isn't that right Dee?"

"Whats wi the jelly. I thought we were makin a fertiliser bomb." The confused Whitey asked.

"A mix bomb won't blow without a detonating charge. That's why ya use a wee bit a jelly - ta detonate it." Answered the knowledgeable wee Desi.

Dee looked at them both, then to the heavens for guidance. He could not find any.

"It's goin rain again." He groaned. "I'm goin to the bog for a pish. Whitey go you and put the kettle on. Desi grab that bag of stuff there and getit inside outa the rain."

Five minutes later they were sitting around a blue Formica topped table drinking mugs of tea and smoking.

"Christ. It was heavy enough that ou bag". Said wee Desi.

"Dee – are you sure we're alright smoking in here wi that gear beside us." Asked a nervous Whitey – he was looking at the paper bag sitting on the fourth and last chair at the table as if it was an unwanted guest.

"Were ye not listenin to the wee man here?" Dee answered indicating wee Desi with his cigarette. "It won't blow without the jelly init. An the jelly won't blow wi out the det init. An the det won't blow unless it has the fuse in it. An the fuse won't do anything until ya light it. Now let's get down to business." So the other two pulled the chairs a bit closer to the older man as he continued.

"The unit from up the road are goin sort us two cars out. When the smokie is ready we'll bring one of the cars up the entry and load it inta it. People'll take less notice of us loadin a bin inta a car up the entry. Then I'll lead in the other car to the target and you two follow me in the car wi the smokie. Whose gona drive yous"?

"I'm a good driver. I'll drive". Said a cocky Whitey.

"Will I be carryin a rod then?" asked wee Desi.

"No. You'll be lightin the fuse. Anyway I'm carrying." Replied Dee as he lifted his pullover to show the shiny black handle of an automatic pistol sticking out of the waistband of his jeans.

"Fook. Oh! sorry Dee. - But were you carryin that when we came down the road?"

"Yep. An keep yer eye on that ou cursin. It's every second word Whitey uses. Don't be getting like him."

"Christ the Brits passed us half a dozen times this morning. If they'd searched us we'd bin fooked. Oh, sorry about the cursin Dee"

"Well. You know that's what we're about wee man. Takin chance. An we cannot do a job like this wi' outa weapon - just in case we need it."

"What ya mean I'll be litin the fuse. I've never lit a fuse before."

"Dead easy. How did ya light that fag there ya have in your gob there?"

"I struck a match."

"See wee man. You're a genius. That's how ya blow a bomb. Strike a match. Then yas jump inta my motor and we'll scoot."

Suddenly there was a loud, and not to be ignored, knock on the front door. Dee immediately pulled the gun from his jeans and cocked it - like an expert and super experienced cop in Kojak. The other two looked at him with horror. Again the door thundered for attention.

"I'll sus it." Said Dee. As he stood up he put the hand with gun in it behind his back. Cautiously he moved towards the front door. The gun was still cocked and he had his finger on the trigger. Desi and Whitey were frozen – and struck dumb. It did not matter what was going to happen next – they were in no way going to be able to influence events in any way.

"Hello whose there?" Dee said as he got to the front door. By now he had the gun clasped in both hands – held in outstretched arms pointed at chest height at the front door

"Ding Dong – Avon calling." Was the response from outside.

Followed by. "Who the Fook do ya tink it is?"

It wasn't a Belfast voice. It was a countryman's voice – thick and rough.

Dee uncocked the pistol and put the safety on before he put the gun back down the waist band of his jeans. He turned to the two young men behind him and hissed lowly, "Now shape up you two."

He opened the door and in stepped a tall and slender man. He was dressed in a greenish tweed suit and even had a tweed tie knotted around the collar of a crisp white shirt. He was carrying a large brown briefcase which matched his shiny brown brogues. Wee Desi whispered to Whitey, "He looks like fookin Dr.Finlay."

"Who's fookin Dr.Finlay?" Was the hushed reply.

Before wee Desi could explain it was a TV show about a Scottish doctor Dee had pushed himself and the new arrival past them both and into the kitchen.

"I think it must a bin stored somewhere wet Countryman. It seems a wee bit damp." Dee said, trying to cover Whitey's mistake, as they followed behind him and the Countryman into the kitchen.

"Nope. I know where it was stored and it was'nee damp. I think youse twats left it out'na the rain last night. Let's have a wee duke at it."

He took a handsome bone-handled pen knife from his pocket and snapped it open. The blade was bright and sliced easily into the thick paper of the bag. He put a hand in and lifted a handful of the white powder out and rubbed it between his fingers.

"I've seen worse." He said and turned around and asked them if there was an electric fire in the house.

"Upstairs." Said Whitey.

"Well now son don't hang around – go and get it." Said the Countryman and turned to wee Desi and told him to empty the contents of the bag onto the floor.

Wee Desi gaped at him before saying "Wh- why?"

"Because ah just told ya to. That why."

It was only then that he turned to Dee and greeted him. "How ya doin Dee? A havnee seen ya since the last time"

"I'm doin alright. Stayin low and movin fast – know whata mean. How 's the cow business? Moo'in along alright?" Dee laughed at his own joke.

"Ha Ha. You city boys are a geg. Geniuses all aren't ye." He replied lifting his eyebrows cynically as he nodded towards the industrious wee Desi kneeling on the floor and doing as instructed. Whitey rushed in with the old and badly dented electric fire. The woven cover on the lead was so old and worn it was hairy as an old rope. He was about to hand the fire to the Countryman when he cut Whitey short saying.

"Jasus don't be given me the filthy thing. Plug it in and set on a chair in the middle of the floor so it can dry the bloody stuff."

Both Whitey and wee Desi, who stopped what he was doing, looked at the Countryman as if he was a maniac.

"Are you jokin mister? What if it sets it off?" said wee Desi from where he knelt like penitent at the Countryman's feet.

"As I said Dee – geniuses.?" Smirked the Countryman..

Whitey grinned and turning to plug in the fire laughed. "Keep your pencil outa the way and we'll be sound wee Desi."

"What's that about?" Asked the Countryman.

"A bit of craic from earlier." Replied Dee.

"Well miss," said the Countryman to Whitey's back, indicating Whitey's long locks to the other two, "when you have the fire goin ya can get down on the floor and help your friend to spread the gear out."

"Do you want a cuppa tay?" Dee asked the Countryman as wee Desi sniggered at Whitey being called "miss".

"Naw. We'd better get this bag outa here and into the other room to prepare it – just in case they do set the kitchen on fire." The Countryman said as indicating his briefcase.

Wee Desi couldn't help himself and blurted out "Why is there money in it?"

" Oh! Jasus this is getting worse," laughed the Countryman as he walked towards the front room, " it has the jelly and the det in it ya numbskull."

Whitey laughed out loud and breathlessly gasped. "Now ya need to get yer pencil out wee Desi."

In the front room the Countryman set his bag down on a spindly wooden coffee table which balanced precariously in the centre of a threadbare rug. He then sat down on the well worn armchair beside it. His tweed suit nearly matched the rough fabric of the chair. He took off his jacket and carefully laid it over the arm of the chair – before he did this he took a pencil from the jacket' s inside pocket.

" I suppose you're carryin Dee." He asked as he laid the jacket down.

" You mean do I have a weapon on me – course I do."

" I don't like guns."

"You told me that the last time Countryman – an I don't like jelly, an smokies - too dangerous. But we gotta do what we gotta do." laughed Dee.

Then the Countryman opened his bag and took out a role of what looked like thin black rope – it was cortex fuse wire – and a pair of pliers, a tape measure, a pair of rubber gloves, black sticky tape, a small wooden box and a red tin lunch box. He pulled on the rubber gloves and handed the tin box to Dee saying, "That's the jelly. Now be careful with it"

"As you mentioned earlier Countryman, I've done it before". Replied Dee, with a put on brogue and a dirty look. Making no reply The Countryman pushed his hands into the rubber gloves and then he opened the wooden box and took out one shiny detonator of a bed of cotton wool before carefully closing it again and securing the lid with its attached brass clasp.

"I don't know the target for this Dee. How long do you want the fuse to be?"

"Let me see – if they light it in the car - then park it and yell a warning - long enough for people to get off side, – probably five minutes."

"Hokey dokey." The Countryman replied and began to measure the cortex with the tape measure.

"About there'll do it". He said as he snipped off about 12 inches of the cortex with the pliers, then he lifted his jacket and fished about in a pocket and retrieved a box of matches. He took four of the safety matches and using his lovely bone handled pen knife he partially split one end of the cortex and inserted the four matches lengthwise right into it, side by side, until only their brown heads protruded from the top like small heads all together in the one sleeping bag.

Then he secured them in place using a very thin piece of the sticky tape which he also cut with his keen knife. Then he pushed the other end of the cortex into the top of the detonator and with the pair of pliers quickly crimped the metal of the detonator securely around the cortex. It was like a long and thin black leg in a tight shiny sock.

He asked Dee for the lunch box back and took out from it what looked like a thick roll of brown fudge wrapped in thick grease proof paper. Using his pencil as a probe he pushed it into the fudge and then forced the detonator with its attached length of cortex into the hole made by the pencil. Then he squeezed the fudge around the hole - tight against the protruding cortex to make sure it was secure.

"I hate the smell of jelly." Said Dee turning his nose up.

"Aw nah! It's gorgeous." Replied Countryman and lifted the roll of fudge-like gelignite up to his nose and inhaled the sickly marzipan odour. Then he used the sticky tape to wrap around his handiwork and make it all tight and secure. He took the tape measure and checked the length of the cortex from the matches at its end to where it was attached to the gelignite.

"Just being cautious here Dee. I don't want you boys blowing your own arses off. You have at least five minutes – if it was me I'd allow myself four maximum – to be sure, to be sure - to be damn sure - ya know."

"Boy – that didn't take ya long."

"New – sure its nay bother to me now. Here keep it in this ou'lunch box until you are ready to put it into the mix. I'll leave here on this wee coffee table for ya. Better not in the same room as the mix. Will ya hav aluk at how the 2 geniuses are getting on next door while I pack up?"

In the kitchen the oil-clothed floor was now totally covered by the pure white powder. It was inches deep in places and glistened like fresh snow in the orange light of the old electric fire.

"Jasas – luks like there's bin a blizzard."

The two young men gawked up at him from where they were hunkered on the floor moving the powder about with their bare hands.

"This is some craic Dee. Unhh?" Grinned Whitey. "Just like playin on the beach."

"Well yer mans got the detonating charge ready. He'll be in for a luk at this in a min-."

"Here he is, " said the Countryman over Dee's shoulder, " youse are doing rightly there lads. Just keep moving it around to let the air at it and the heat from the dirty wee fire will get ta work on it. Another wee while will sort it. - Well I 'll be goin then – are ya sure you will get the mix right Dee?"

" No bother Countryman, I've done it before. As we have already established." Dee fired him another dirty look. The Countryman grinned back at him – happy his remark had found it's mark.

"OK then, - don't forget - keep the jelly and the mix separate until the last minute – good luck for the job then boys. Try not to be dying for the cause now – won't yas."

Dee let the Countryman out and watched him stride smartly up the street - he did not look back. He looks like a tick-man - with that briefcase and his cocky dander - thought Dee as he closed the front door.

"Right boys let's get started. First thing is another drop o' tay. I'll stick the kettle on again and you two keep spreadin the gear."

Soon enough Dee was sitting at the kitchen table again, supping a steaming mug of tea and smoking leisurely on a long Benson and Hedges.

"Right now don't be tearin the arse out of it you two. I know youse are workin hard at dryin the stuff but come on – youse can have a wee break. And have a smoke and this tay a made for yiss – before its freezin."

" I'm still not sure if you should be smoking near that stuff." Said Whitey nodding down at the white and glistening floor. Wee Desi, his earlier cockiness long since fled, said nothing but his concerned face clearly showed he agreed with Whitney's comment.

" Christ yas ar two big girls blouses – here take these." Said Dee setting his own cigarette over the table's edge so as the glowing tip was away from the table top – but the red hot end was directly above the white powder on the floor. Carelessly Dee took two cigarettes from the gold coloured pack and flipped them both into his mouth and lit them with a match.

As he handed one to each of his companions he said "Watch this" – and threw the still flaming match into the middle of the fertiliser on the floor. He giggled as the other two nearly fell over each other in a rush for the door. Before they had reached it the match flared briefly, spluttered and then died.

" Will you two ballickses catch yerselfs on. It is not going to do anything – it's still too wet to even smoulder and it will not explode without the det an jelly and the rest of the mix."

They sheepishly took his proffered cigarettes and sat down. Wee Desi took a swill of tea and then had a long drag of his B&H. As he blew the smoke out in a long breath he said cockily. "We had Whitey shittin them there Dee didn't we. You throwin that match into the gear. Cracker"

The other two looked at him for a minute before Whitey gultered out as he began laughing.

"Fook me you're a fookin chancer Wee Desi."

Spluttering with laughter Dee said " Now Whitey cut out the cursin – but Jasus – you're right. You're a chanchin bastard wee man." As he cuffed Wee Desi on the back of his head with his hand.

" Ye' s are right. I was brickin it too." The wee man laughed. Soon the three of them were laughing away together each with a mug of tea in one hand and a long ,smoking cigarette in the other - and a ½ hundredweight of fertiliser spread around their feet. When they had finished the tea, and another couple of fags each, Dee got to his feet and said.

"Let's get the show on the road boys. Whitey you go and find an empty bin. Chancer – oh! Sorry I mean wee Desi. Go you up the road and see Brick, he'll have the two cars for us. The rest of the mix will be in one o them. Drive it nice and slowly down to here so as nobody notices ya - then park it in the next street and bring the rest of the mix round to me. It'll be in a haversack in the boot. Brick will bring the other car down and park it in the same street and then he'll give ya its keys

Desi replied. " Who's Brick, Dee - and where will he be?"

"You know Brick!"

"Naw – don't."

"Big Alan McClay – McCLAY! Brick! - Get it"

"Ah. Yes. I know who ya mean now – but I don't get it."

"They make bricks from clay – he is named McClay - so he gets Brick. Now hurry up. – And check there's petrol in it"

"Do you think I'm stupid Dee?"

Dee cocked his head to one side and looked at him as if he was a naughty child. Desi grasped the sarcasm in the look, just grunted and headed down the hall and out of the door, slamming it hard behind him. The house shook.

"Now Whitey you go and git a bin."

"No probs Dee. One trash can coming up. Adi oats"

"Whata da say?"

"Trash can Dee. That's what they call them in the flix."

"Naw. Not that - the other thing."

"Oh! Adi oats. And that's what they say in the cowboy movies Dee. Its cowboy for goodbye."

"Jasus Whitey how'd you get inta this army. The correct word is Adios. And its Mexican. Ah! Frig I don't care anymore. Just get the damn bin – an remember - THIS ain't a bloody movie."

Away Whitey went, out the back door. He rattled the house too.

"Christ – those two are noisy buggers." Dee said to the empty kitchen.

Two minutes later the kitchen door was thrown open again and an exuberant Whitey rushed in. " Sorted Dee, sorted. Ah gotta a trash can – sorry Dee. A bin, I gotta bin."

"How could ya? Ya just went out."

"Observation Dee – observation, that's how. Sure ma uncle's bin was out in the yard. Did YOU, - not notice it?"

"God help me! You are daft Whitey an ya'll get us all stuck in jail."

"Unhh?"

"Come on." Ordered Dee as he headed out to the yard where the bin stood in the middle - like a dirty silver truncated marble pillar.

"Where's the rubbish Whitey?"

"Ah dumped it in the alley."

"Ay – sure nobody' ll notice it lying there in the middle of the entry. Of course they won't! And tell me Whitey what's that on the side of the bin?"

Whitey looked at Dee as if he did not understand the question, eventually he caught on and replied.

"The number and the address of the house Dee - sure that's so as the binmen know where to bring it back too." he explained.

"That's right Whitey. And if we blow the bin to smithereens and they find the bit of the bin wi' the writin on it they'll come here – to investigate. Now get out of my sight an get a bin from at least three streets away – and put that rubbish you left in the entry back into the bin"

"Awk I'm sorry Dee I'll get right onto it." Whitey said sheepishly as he slipped out the entry door and headed off. When he had the house to himself Dee sat down and had another cigarette. Whitey was back first – about an hour later. At least he had the sense to come up the entry with the empty bin. It was pretty decrepit, only one handle and dented nearly shapeless. Years ago someone had roughly painted the number forty onto it but the black mark was fading now. Dee made more tea while Whitey again started spreading the nearly drying fertiliser around on the floor again. By now the kitchen was very warm because the electric fire had been going for so long. Wee Desi arrived a while later, huffing and puffing under the weight of the rucksack.

"The cars are parked a couple a streets away like ya said Dee."

"Right, " said Dee as he picked some fertiliser up and rubbed it between his fingers, " its dry now - let's get it mixed". Ordered Dee as they emptied the rucksack, which contained about twenty packets of sugar. They began tearing the sugar bags open and piling the sugar into the middle of floor on top of the fertiliser.

"The handy thing about these wee bags of sugar is the weight is marked on the side and then you know exactly how many bags are needed for the mix to be just right. Now let's just make sure it is all mixed nicely together". Explained Dee as they all knelt together on the floor moving the whole lot around with their hands until it was all one white mass of powder.

"That's us boys". Said Dee when he was satisfied. "Now let's get it all into the bin and pack it down as hard as we can". So they started to shovel it into the bin. Eventually after a bit of huffing and puffing all the mix was in the bin. Dee insisted the floor was as clear as they could possibly make it of all traces of the explosive powder. He even got them to fetch a bucket and mop and wash it. The oil cloth changed colour from its previous grey to a washed out blue.

Then they took to turns to stamp it down – that is they took turns to stand inside the bin and jump up and down on the powder. As each of them took a turn to do this one of the others held their hand to help balance the stamper - it was all a bit of a laugh.

"This how they make wine ya know." Dee informed them.

"What? – From fertiliser?" asked an astonished Whitey.

"Are ya daft? From sugar." giggled a perceptive wee Desi.

"Yas are both eejits," laughed Dee, " this is how they squeeze the juice outa the grapes."

"I never drink wine." offered Whitey – as if this was a feasible reason for not knowing about the fine art of winemaking. Pretty soon the bin was three quarters full. And ready to be a bomb – all it needed was a fuse laden detonator rammed into it.

"More tea, and a fag for me. You two are going to get things movin. And then we go and blow this place to bits." Said Dee.

"What's the target Dee?" wee Desi asked.

"The Daily News print works. Those bastards are spewing out lies about us every day" Dee replied as put the kettle on for the umpteenth time.

"Now you two go and get one of the cars and bring it up the entry to the back door. But before yous get the car lift the bin - carefully - out into the entry. That way we'll have less muckin about to do when Whitey brings the car up. I'll put the detonating charge into the mix outside - just before we go. Once that's in there'll be no smoking in the car – unless yas want ta blow yerselves to kingdom come. Then drop me off at the getaway car and I'll be right behind yas all the way. So have a fag now. And no tootin horns to let me know you've arrived. Just come in – through the back door - and get me"

The house shook – as they went out the front door– leaving Dee to enjoy a cuppa and a quiet smoke. Twenty minutes later and Dee was getting twitchy. They should have been well back by now. I'll smoke this fag and then go and look for them he thought. A couple of minutes later - as he was stubbing it out someone began furiously knocking on the front door. Like a cat springing for prey he whipped the pistol out of his waistband and was down the hall by the door. They've been scooped he thought.

"Yes. Who is there?" he asked through the door – in what he thought was a nice polite voice.

"It's us Dee. Quickly – open up." they called out together. Dee carefully put the gun back down his waistband as, continuing his ruse of being a normal householder he gently said " OK now. I'll just be a moment."

When he opened the door they stumbled in and he slammed it closed behind them.

"Jasas – this better be good or I'll shoot you two eejits. What kept yas? And the back. Yous were ta come the back door." he shouted.

"We cud'nt get up the entry in the car." they blurted out.

" Ya cud getta a bus up that big entry. Can neither of drive properly or what?"

"The binmen Dee. The binmen and the bin lorry are in the entry."

"Wh – what? Ah! Fook no. Fook no." Dee squealed in reply as the three of them rushed down the hall and out the back.

As they tumbled into the entry a massive binman dropped a bin, clanging and empty at their feet. It was a well dented bin with only one handle. The number forty was scrawled on its side in black paint.

" Are yous all right fellahs? Yous luk like yas hav' seen a ghost." said the giant binman.

"Yous need a new bin. That ou ones fallen ta bits. And what was in it – t'was bloody heavy ta lift, an awkward too, with only one handle. Well see yas again then." he cheerily said as he followed the lorry down the entry.

"Fook. Fook. Fook." Dee said as the bin lorry, with its 56lb. of fertiliser and sugar mix rumbled on down the entry. Whitey and wee Desi both had the same thought.

"No need for that ou cursin Dee." Luckily they were both smart - or scared – enough, to say nothing.

"At least it can't explode without the detonating charge." said wee Desi with a sense of relief. Dee cuffed him, lightly, on the back of the head and said. "Fook up wee Desi!"

*This story is based loosely on a real life incident related to me by a former participant in Belfast's recent civil conflict.

BRIGHT RIPPLES
IN A DARK POOL

*"oscail do shúile d'iontas na cruinne"**

Anon.

old irish saying – "open your eyes to the wonders of the universe"

BRIGHT RIPPLES IN A DARK POOL

My Granda was a solitary man.

Of course I had no real conception of that when I was young. He being my Daddy's daddy was a difficult enough reality to grasp.

He was one of the people who surrounded me - fortunate child that I was - with love and security.

On reflection I now realise that he often brought me to solitary places - that is solitary - not sad - because he was not sad, nor were our times together - for he played, and joked, and sang, and taught to me, and with me – even when we visited the cemetery. His hand had always seemed to be upon me, ruffling my hair, holding me by the hand, resting on my meagre shoulder, always reassuring me that when I was with him I was protected. He did nod and greet many people, but he had no real friends that I knew off. But he always seemed happy.

I now realise that he had a special belief, held faithfully inside himself. I believe it was that which kept him smiling.

He lived by himself a little bit out of the city. It was an old cottage with dull, cement finished walls. When my Daddy was very young there had been neither electricity nor running water when they lived there. They had used oil lamps for light and fetched water from a hand pump at the end of the lane. By the time I was born most of that had changed and Granda even had central heating in now.

Visits to the local cemetery were regular. He showed me where his parents and grandparents were buried and when we were there we always stood quietly for a moment by their graves. We bowed our heads and prayed. My prayers sincere, as the prayers of all children are, useless of course, but sincere none the less. Then we would clamber over the graves and he would read out the names and the dates - running a commentary all the time "That's an old one 1848". "Isn't the carving wonderful on this one" "I went to school with the fellah in that one. He was a good footballer but mean as a swarm of bees – a bit of a bully. Well he's no one to bully now."

One of the reasons he brought me to there was to watch the rabbits. He would pull me down low behind a headstone and shush me. And, if the place was still and quiet, out they would come - from beneath all the bushes about the place. There were dozens of them, and after they had nervously looked all around themselves they would start nibbling the grass between the graves - and any fresh flowers left on the graves. "If we had a good catapult we could get one for making rabbit stew with." He always said that, he knew it annoyed me, and then we would laugh quietly into our hands at the thought of it.

Before long he would say. "Jasus I have to get up. My knees are killing me - crouched down like this. Are you ready to surprise the wee buggers? - 1, 2 – 3 - jump!"

And we would both leap into the air shouting and waving our hands and laughing as the rabbits shot off, terrified, in all directions.

One day there were more rabbits than we had seen for a long time and Granda suggested waiting a bit longer to allow more to come out. He moaned about his knees the whole time until he could stick it no longer and quickly counted out the 1 -2 -3 -- jump. As usual we yelled and shrieked and the rabbits began to scatter, like spit off a hot skillet, but as they were darting off a loud scream ripped out and vibrated across the graves.

We became as still as the headstones. The rabbits of course kept running.

"Jasus!" Granda exclaimed, "There's an ou' lady down there near that big marble crypt. We must have scared the devil out of her." Then he began to giggle, struggling hard to suppress it.

"I had better see how she is. Come on. And don't be laughin!" He choked the order out through his giggles.

And so we went down, and he apologised and explained what we had been doing. Turns out he had known her late husband, but he did not know he was dead. He offered to buy her a cup of tea at the nearby shopping centre, she declined and smiling forgivingly and said. "Some other time maybe. I'm fine now – but you can imagine what I thought when I saw you two leaping about and yelling."

He made me promise not to tell my Daddy. I never, ever did.

He lived alone – but my Granny was not dead. When I was that age she was not anything. I was never told what she was – all I knew was that she was never there.

There was just a plain and dark wood frame displaying a lonely photograph of a pretty looking young woman on the mantelpiece. Most summer days there was a flower posy from the garden lying, bound with some long grass stems, beside her picture. I little realised in those days that this was his homage to her. But to me she was always just a whisper. And when I appeared the whisper became a loud – and now I realise obvious – diversion, about the weather, or the news, or anything that entered their heads.

The place he took me most often was a nearly grown over lane near the back of his house. He called it Biddy's Lane and it was green. Green grass the whole way, and tall green hedges, which commanded the surrounding world to be quiet. It was here we stopped to listen to the birds in the hedge, and the humming summer insects. He named the birds to me, the tiny wren, the bombastic little robin, the blousy bullfinch, the flighty blue tit, and the crows and thrushes. His favourites were the black cock blackbird, dark and handsome with its eyes of bright gold - like the shining ear-rings on the black face of a pirate. And it's poor mate - brown - and dull as dust. And he gave me all their Irish names too, like Ri Rua, which means red king and this bird is better named in Irish than in English for it is the scarlet little chaffinch. He taught me other Irish words – like, slan, for goodbye, and plubernacht. Plubernacht was a word I loved and I loved being plubernacht for it means soggy and wet, and he often got us both soggy and wet. At times he was more of a tumbling boisterous boy than I.

Here in Biddy's Lane we picked raspberries, hiding like rubies midst the thorns in the jungle of the hedgerow. And he explained to me the seasons as the lane changed its face and the raspberries became blackberries. We even battled down through Biddy's when the silvered brambles struggled under the glistening weight of untouched snow.

He always brought me back dirty, and wet, and like I had been pulled through a hedge back ways – and often I had been.

But he always brought me back deliriously happy. But no matter how happy I was there was always something missing. When quite young I did not know what it was. As I got older I knew – but I was also afraid to mention it. And when older still I knew it was better not to mention it.

The whisper – the Granny who was never there, the Granny who was not dead, the Granny they never talked about in front of me. I loved my Granda and I knew I would love her too. But Granny was a word I became afraid to say.

At the bottom of Biddy's Lane there was a large pond. And it was to here that we always made our way. He never took me to Biddy's without ending up down at the edge of the pond. It was surrounded with low bushes and impoverished willow trees, small - and more wilting - than elegantly drooping. The water was always dark and rarely seemed to catch the sky on its surface. When here we would sit and watch for the rising of invisible fish, and sometimes he would bring bread and scatter it across the glossy black surface to entice the never seen rudd and roach to break the surface for the treat he had thrown. The pond had a smell all of its own, slightly peaty and a hint of vegetation, vegetation past its best. But it was always still, dark, and slightly threatening. He fished here as a boy he told me – but give up because the rudd and roach never seemed to get any bigger.

It was here he give me my nickname.

One day he skipped a stone over the jet surface; it flew with barely a sound or a splash, and he said, "Look. Look at the ripples from the stone. See how they catch the blue sky. Never forget – even the darkest pool has bright ripples. Just like you."

"What do you mean like me Granda?" I asked.

"Because you are one of my bright ripples. - And that's what I will call from now on – Rip."

And so from then he - and then eventually everyone else - just called me Rip.

I was about 13 when I asked him. "Granda you once told me I was one of your bright ripples. Have you other bright ripples?"

He answered me casually. "Well your Mammy and Daddy are bright ripples to me."

"Is that all?" I asked.

Now he seemed a little uneasy, "Well a nice cup of tea. An ya know I love a wee drink down at the bar - and watchin a match on TV. And watchin the world around me – especially when you are with me. Every one needs their bright ripples Rip. Simple things ya know. Simple things."

My next question seemed to hit him like a thump to the head.

"Granda. Why am I not allowed to talk about Granny? Why do you and Daddy not talk about her when I am there?"

He steadied himself, and then said. "We do. We do. We talk about her all the time."

"Not to me."

"Well. – Well, you're a bit young."

"Not anymore Granda."

And he looked right at me and said. "No. No not anymore. Jasus look at the size of ya."

"Well is Granny one of your bright ripples?"

"Aye Rip. She is. -- Maybe the brightest of all."

And he started to weep, ever so slightly and as he rubbed his face with the back of his rough sleeve he said. "Your Da'll be waitin - lets head back."

And that night I asked my Daddy to tell me about his Mammy. He too looked like he had been thumped in the in the face. "Well – well," he said, obviously playing for time.

"Well - where do I start? – I don't remember much about my Mammy. She just went away – that's all - she went away. Maybe my Da should talk to you about it all Rip. He stays in touch with her more than me. He will never ever stop lovin her ya know. He talks about her every time I see him."

"How does he stay in touch – does he phone her up? Is she in England like Auntie Margaret?"

"No she is not in England. She is in hospital. He goes to see her in hospital. Three times a week he goes."

"Then can I go and see her? I went to see you when you were in hospital."

"It's not like that Rip. I was having a wee operation. Your Granny is sick in a different way. Long ago something happened to her and she just forgot everything. She forgot who I was, - who Granda was. She even forgot who she was. She stopped eating and washing herself. Granda could not leave her on her own and he had to go to work - and look after me too. I was little then, a lot younger than you are now. Hospital was the only place she was safe and could be looked after properly."

"If she doesn't know anybody why does Granda visit her so often?"

"Because he loves her – and he thinks that one day she will get better. He keeps hoping she will remember him - and then he will be able to bring her home."

Mammy had been standing against the doorframe, with her head tipped to one side and her arms folded, her blue woollen cardigan rolled up to her elbows while we were talking. He kept looking up at her, as if for approval as he spoke to me. I always remember the look on her face; it was a sort of mixture of sadness and kindness. She smiled down at me and just said.

"It's very sad Rip. Isn't it?"

The next time I saw Granda I told him I knew about Granny. He was not surprised and I realised Daddy had probably filled him in about our conversation. We dandered down to the cemetery and chatted about it. There was no scaring the rabbits that day as we just kept walking along. He did not tell me much more than I already knew, then he said, "I am going to bring you somewhere special – somewhere you and I haven't been before – let's go."

He took me down Biddy's Lane and past the pond, towards the big lough. Here the ground was marshy, so we headed through the marshy ground to a little rise in the midst of this soggy peat land. On the little rise there was a stout, yet stunted, birch tree, its branches scraggy and nearly leafless – it was like a claw reaching to the sky. Then he showed me where he had carved, a long time ago, his name inside a heart - along with Granny's name - into the tree's bronze skin. And as he showed it to me his eyes glistened, wet with sadness.

"We were both only sixteen when we did that. Some think a tree like this - on its own little hillock - is a fairy tree. Awk sure ya know that anyway. Well someone had told us that if we carved our names on a fairy tree on Samweeon eve night our souls would be together for eternity. It was a cold winter that year and the night we came was freezin. The frost glistened like silver dust under a sliver of a new moon and the sky was glorious. In those days there was little light pollution out here and so we could see the luminous dark blue of the night sky and how it was studded with countless stars - and the Milky Way! It was ghostly and beautiful. Sure we hardly ever see it now wi the dirt in the sky and all those oul lights. But we were foundered, as by the light of a thumb of a candle I guided her shivering hand as she carved my name. I thought it would always be like that – her and me - together forever. Well it brought no luck to her and me. But I feel close to her here. Even when I am with her in the hospital I do not feel as close to her as I feel here. Sure we were no more than children when we cut that tree – but we were special – her and I. We were special. And I will always be with her when I sit here with the bog cotton nodding all about me in the wind." And he swung his hand around to indicate the white fluffy bog cottons, dancing to the wind, in the soggy ground around us.

I took him by the hand and led us both back, our feet squelching in the soft ground, as we headed the cottage. We did not speak the whole way back.

I loved him more that day than I ever had before. And I loved her too.

As I got older I spend less time with him. There was so much studying to do and I had hurling and football matches play. But on the other hand I was able to ride my bike out to his place, or take the bus. I no longer had to wait on him picking me up, or my Da dropping me off.

One Saturday I was supposed to play a hurling match but it was cancelled so I headed off to see him. He was not at the cottage when I arrived so I waited around for a while but when he did not appear I went off to look for him. I headed to Biddy's first, it was hard riding the bike through the long swinging grass and when I got to the pond there was no sign of him. I rode back to the cottage to see if he had returned but he was not there so I headed for home.

A the house Mammy came out when she heard me and threw her arms around me. That scared me – I knew she was going to tell me something awful.

"Oh Rip. We had a phone call from your Granda. Just after you left for your match. He was very upset because he got word your Granny died in hospital this morning."

"Awk Mammy no! No. I was out here to see him and he wasn't there. Where is he now? Has he gone to the hospital?" I said.

"No. He was crying, heartbroken, on the phone and said he could not bear to go. He asked your Daddy to go the hospital."

"I will have to go back. I have to find him Mammy."

"No Rip wait until Daddy gets back. He will not be much longer."

"No Mammy – I have to find him."

"Rip come back – come back." She shouted after me as I pedalled off – back the way I had come. My was heart bursting out of my breast with fear as I pedalled furiously back to Grandas. I knew this was going to get worse. I had a dread. In my mind the whole way back I could see the menacing black water of the pond down Biddy's lane. I could see him floating there; face down and dead in the dark pool. The brightest hope in his life was gone. He had been faithful for so long. So sure she would return to him. Hope is often a cruel virtue, a virtue without charity. It had buoyed him up for so long only to be dashed – oh! Granda don't do anything stupid.

As I got closer to Biddy's the panic rose inside me. Oh Granda! I am coming – I am coming.

It started to rain as I reached Biddy's and forced the bike through the long grass. The pond was still - save for the ripples from the raindrops making curving patterns all across its bleak surface. They ran into each other catching a little of the grey sky on their round edges as they moved. There was no other movement. Nothing floated on the water. I cannot remember if that scared me more or reassured me. Maybe he had sunk beneath the surface. I dared to hope – and then remembered despairingly - he had hoped.

There was no hope.

This day would only get worse.

I was not sure what to do next. Should I head to his cottage or go back home? I turned to go back down the lane when I realised there was another place to look.

The birch tree in the bog - near the loughshore. I set the bike down and headed for the soft ground through the bog cottons. The rain had eased a little but the sky was eerily dark and portentous. Suddenly the day seemed to snarl. It was as if it was night-time – not as dark as night, but – unknown, threatening, that was the word which said it - threatening. And I was more terrified than I had ever been in my life. And I was cold, for the air had fallen cool all around. I squelched my way through the bog, my passage was the only noise to be heard – there was no wind, for the bog cottons stood as still and straight as soldiers. No birds called and not an insect winged about me. I remember well the world had lost colour, everything was just shades of grey, like an old movie, and a mist was starting to form – low and still over the sodden ground.

***

Suddenly – low and far off in the distance I heard my name being shouted. I t was coming from behind me, I could not make out who was calling and though I stood for a moment trying to place the voice I soon pressed on. The surrounding mist was rising quickly and was soon was to my shoulders.

Then in front I saw the small hummock of slightly higher ground - with its claw of a half dead bog-birch. It was like a small desert island sitting on its sea of grey mist. And then I realised there was a figure by the tree. It was a man - silhouetted against a soft golden glow which seemed to be coming from the tree. I stopped. Frightened - to go on.

The glow grew stronger – as I watched I began to recognise the figure – it was my Daddy.

And in the strengthening golden light his features started to become clear, he was smiling at someone, and nodding. I heard nothing as he mouthed words back to unknown person, then a hand reached for him and gently touched his face. The other person was on the other side of the tree from me.

Then in shock I dropped to my knees in the moss and peat.

It was not my Daddy – It was Granda – only he was young, younger than my Daddy was at that time.

The other figure stepped from behind the tree, only, it seemed more like she stepped from out of the tree's trunk – for it was a woman – and I knew her too, from the photo in the cottage, she was more beautiful than her black and white picture could ever have shown. They both turned towards me – they knew I was there – I was no longer afraid. I was seeing something wonderful – unbelievable – but so wonderful. He waved at me and smiled lovingly, and she waved too. And then I heard his voice "I was waiting on you Rip. I could not leave without saying slan leat. This is something to see – eh me boyo! I love you. Be happy for me. For us. Tell yer Da all about. He won't believe you ya know." and with that he put an arm around her shoulder and blew me a long kiss with his other - hand then they both stepped into the tree. The golden glow began to fade. Around me the mist too was disappearing as the sky brightened. I tingled with a joy I could not understand, and I was no longer cold. I was crying and yet beaming a smile that nearly hurt my cheeks.

**

Meanwhile the other voice was still calling me and it was much closer now. This time it was my Daddy and as I turned from where I still knelt in the soggy ground he reached me and grabbed me to him.

"What are you doing here? Why are you laughing? - And crying? Are you all right son? What is going on? Who was talking to you there?"

"I am so happy Daddy. He knew I would come. He was waiting for me so as he could say slan."*

"Who?"

"Granda – he has gone. She came back for him. Don't cry Daddy, its all right" I said for he had started to weep a little.

"Rip – I know you are upset and this is hard for you to understand at only fourteen. But you have to keep a clear head because we have to find Granda. I am worried about him because he is so upset. We all are. This is a difficult day for us all"

"But he is over there Daddy. Look." He followed my gaze to the tree.

"Da. Da."

He shouted over to the figure sitting against the tree as we went over to him. But there was no reply.

He looked like he had just fallen asleep against the small, fat trunk.

But he had gone.

And I had never seen him look happier. He loved us – but he wanted to be with her.

It took a while for my Daddy to finally understand.

*Irish for bye, cheerio.